Hezekiah Butterworth

Songs of History

Poems and Ballads Upon Important Episodes in American History

Hezekiah Butterworth

Songs of History
Poems and Ballads Upon Important Episodes in American History

ISBN/EAN: 9783744784139

Printed in Europe, USA, Canada, Australia, Japan

Cover: Foto ©Andreas Hilbeck / pixelio.de

More available books at **www.hansebooks.com**

SONGS OF HISTORY

Poems and Ballads

UPON IMPORTANT EPISODES IN AMERICAN HISTORY

BY

HEZEKIAH BUTTERWORTH

———— ⋆ ————

BOSTON

NEW ENGLAND PUBLISHING COMPANY

1887

PREFACE.

MANY of these poems have appeared in different periodicals. Several were published in "Poems for Christmas, Easter, and New Year's," a holiday volume, and I am indebted to the courtesy of the publishers for their use again. Others were written for music, and are used by the courtesy of John Church & Co. Several were written for special use on American holidays. Others are here used for the first time.

They are brought together in this form in answer to a request that I would compile the verses I had written on subjects associated with American history, a request made in the hope that such a book might prove useful to the teacher, the family, and the school.

It is said that poetry points the morals of history, and interprets the spirit of historic events. It may be well to begin a more sympathetic study of what is poetic in our own national life. In other lands every episode of history, every mountain and river, every trade and occupation, every heroic act and every

3

holiday, has its song, and we may well ask our own land for its meanings, and study together its poetic past. If the verses in this volume fail of their ideals, — and I am well aware of their inadequacy, — I hope that they yet may prove useful in their intention, and may offer some help and direction to minds of larger vision, intuition, and inspiration.

H. B.

28 Worcester St., Boston.

CONTENTS.

SONGS OF HISTORY.

THE THANKSGIVING FOR AMERICA.

BARCELONA, APRIL, 1493.

" Venient annis
Sæcula seris, quibus Oceanus
Vincula rerum laxet, et ingens
Pateat tellus, Typhisque novos
Detegas orbes, nec sit terris
Ultima Thule."

I.

'Twas night upon the Darro.
The risen moon above the shadowy tower
Of Comares shone, the silver sun of night,
And poured its lustrous splendors through the halls
Of the Alhambra.
          The air was breathless,
Yet filled with ceaseless songs of nightingales,
And odors sweet of falling orange blooms;
The misty lamps were burning odorous oil;
The uncurtained balconies were full of life,
And laugh and song, and airy castanets,
And gay guitars.
          Afar Sierras rose,
Domes, towers, and pinnacles, over royal heights,
Whose crowns were gemmed with stars.
          The Generaliffe,

The summer palace of old Moorish kings
In vanished years, stood sentinel afar,
A pile of shade, as brighter grew the moon,
Impearling fountain sprays, and shimmering
On seas of citron orchards cool and green,
And terraces embowered with vernal vines
And breathing flowers.
       In shadowy arcades
Were loitering priests, and here and there
A water-carrier passed with tinkling bells.
       There came a peal of horns,
That woke Granada, city of delights,
From its long moonlight reverie.   Again : —
The suave lute ceased to play, and castanet ;
The water-bearer stopped, and ceased his song
The wandering troubadour.
       Then rent the air
Another joyous peal, and oped the gates
And entered there a train of cavaliers,
Their helmets glittering in the low red moon.
       The streets and balconies
All danced with wondering life.   The train moved on,
And filled the air again the horns melodious,
And loud the heralds shouted : —

*"Thy name, O Fernando, through all earth shall be
    sounded,*
Columbus has triumphed, his foes are confounded."

       A silence followed,
Could such tidings be ?   Men heard and whispered,

Eyes glanced to eyes, feet uncertain moved,
Never on mortal ears had fallen words
Like these.   And was the earth a star?
       On marched the cavaliers,
And pealed again the horns, and again cried
The heralds : —

*" Thy name, Isabella, through all earth shall be sounded;
Columbus has triumphed, his foes are confounded!"* *

       All hearts were thrilled.
" Isabella!"   That name breathed faith and hope
And lofty aim.   Emotion swayed the crowds ;
Tears flowed, and acclamations rose, and rushed
The wondering multitudes towards the plaza.
" Isabella !   Isabella !" it filled
The air — that one word " Isabella !"
       And now
'Tis noon of night.   The moon hangs near the earth —
A golden moon in golden air; the peaks
Like silver tents of shadowy sentinels
Glint 'gainst the sky.   The plaza gleams and surges
Like a sea.   The joyful horns peal forth again,
And falls a hush, and cry the heralds : —

*" Thy name, Isabella, shall be praised by all the living;
Haste, haste to Barcelona, and join the Great Thanks-
    giving!"*

What nights had seen Granada!

        * This couplet is not original.

Yet never one like this !   The moon went down,
And fell the wings of shadow, yet the streets
Still swarmed with people hurrying on and on.

II.

Morn came,
With bursts of nightingales and quivering fires ·
The cavaliers rode forth toward Barcelona.
The city followed, throbbing with delight.
The happy troubadour, the muleteer,
The craftsmen all, the boy and girl, and e'en
The mother — 'twas a soft spring morn ;
The fairest skies of earth those April morns
In Andalusia.   Long was the journey,
But the land was flowers, and nights were not,
And birds sang all the hours, and breezes cool
Fanned all the ways along the sea.
The roads were filled
With hurrying multitudes.   For well 'twas known
That he the conqueror, viceroy of the isles,
Was riding from Seville to meet the king.
And what were conquerors before to him whose eye
Had seen the world a star, and found the star a world ?
Once he had walked
The self-same ways, roofless and poor and sad,
A beggar at old convent doors, and heard
The very children jeer him in the streets,
And ate his crust, and made his roofless bed
Upon the flowers beside his boy, and prayed,
And found in trust a pillow radiant
With dreams immortal.   Now ?

III.

That was a glorious day
That dawned on Barcelona. Banners filled
The thronging towers, the old bells rung, and blasts
Of lordly trumpets seemed to reach the sky
Cerulean. All Spain had gathered there,
And waited there his coming; Castilian knights,
Gay cavaliers, hidalgos young, and e'en the old
Puissant grandees of far Aragon,
With glittering mail, and waving plumes, and all
The peasant multitude with bannerets
And charms and flowers.
                Beneath pavilions
Of brocades of gold, the Court had met.
The dual crowns of Leon old and proud Castile
There waited him, the peasant mariner.
                The trumpets waited
Near the open gates ; the minstrels young and fair
Upon the tapestries and arrased walls,
And everywhere from all the happy provinces
The wandering troubadours.
                Afar was heard
A cry, a long acclaim. Afar was seen
A proud and stately steed with nodding plumes,
Bridled with gold, whose rider stately rode,
And still afar a long and sinuous train
Of silvery cavaliers. A shout arose,
And all the city, all the vales and hills,
With silver trumpets rung.

He came, the Genoese,
With reverent look and calm and lofty mien,
And saw the wondering eyes and heard the cries
And trumpet peals, as one who followed still
Some Guide unseen.

Before his steed
Crowned Indians marched with lowly faces,
And wondered at the new world that they saw;
Gay parrots shouted from their gold-bound arms,
And from their crests swept airy plumes.   The sun
Shone full in splendor on the scene, and here
The old and new world met.   But —

IV.

Hark! the heralds!
How they thrill all hearts and fill all eyes with tears!
The very air seems throbbing with delight;
Hark! hark! they cry, in chorus all they cry: —

"*A Castilla y á Leon, á Castilla y á Leon,*
Nuevo mundo dio Colon!"

Every heart now beats with his,
The stately rider on whose calm face shines
A heaven-born inspiration.   Still the shout:
"*Nuevo mundo dio Colon!*" how it rings!
From wall to wall, from knights and cavaliers,
And from the multitudinous throngs,
A mighty chorus of the vales and hills!
"*A Castilla y á Leon!*"

And now the golden steed
Draws near the throne ; the crowds move back, and
    rise
The reverent crowns of Leon and Castile ;
And stands before the tear-filled eyes of all
The multitudes the form of Isabella.
Semiramis ? Zenobia ? What were they
To her, as met her eyes again the eyes of him
Into whose hands her love a year before
Emptied its jewels !
    He told his tale :
The untried deep, the green Sargasso Sea,
The varying compass, the affrighted crews,
The hymn they sung on every doubtful eve,
The sweet hymn * to the Virgin. How there came

---

* The evening hymn of the crews of Columbus, sung on every
night during the outward voyage, was the *Ave Maris Stella :* —

AVE MARIS STELLA.

Gentle Star of Ocean !
  Portal of the sky !
Ever Virgin Mother
  Of the Lord most high !

Oh ! by Gabriel's Ave,
  Utter'd long ago,
Eva's name reversing,
  'Stablish peace below.

Break the captive's fetters,
  Light on blindness pour,
All our ills expelling,
  Every bliss implore.

The land birds singing, and the drifting weeds,
How broke the morn on fair San Salvador,
How the *Te Deum* on that isle was sung,
And how the cross was lifted in the name
Of Leon and Castile.   And then he turned
His face towards Heaven, "O Queen!   O Queen!
There kingdoms wait the triumphs of the cross!"

v.

Then Isabella rose,
With face illumined : then overcome with joy
She sank upon her knees, and king and court
And nobles rose and knelt beside her,

Show thyself a Mother,
Offer him our sighs,
Who for us Incarnate
Did not thee despise.

Virgin of all Virgins!
To thy shelter take us;
Gentlest of the gentle,
Chaste and gentle make us.

Still as on we journey,
Help our weak endeavor;
Till with thee and Jesus
We rejoice forever.

Through the highest Heaven,
To the Almighty Three,
Father, Son, and Spirit,
One same glory be.

And followed them the sobbing multitude ;
Then came a burst of joy, a chorus grand,
And mighty antiphon —

" *We praise thee, Lord, and, Lord, acknowledge thee,
And give thee glory ! — Holy, Holy, Holy !*"

Loud and long it swelled and thrilled the air,
That first Thanksgiving for the new-found world !

VI.

The twilight roses bloomed
In the far skies o'er Barcelona.
The gentle Indians came and stood before
The throne, and smiled the queen, and said :
" I see my gems again."   The shadow fell,
And trilled all night beneath the moon and stars
The happy nightingales.

TWO CONQUERORS.

I.

GUILLAUME.

I REMEMBER Falaise and the songs that we sung
When eventide gathered the old and the young,
And over the vineyards the golden moon hung,
    In the years that are fled.

My fleet on the waters again I behold,
The gonfalons waving, the pennons of gold,
The three bannered Lions of Normandy old,
    As in years that are fled.

I pointed to England, and proudly behind
The wings of a thousand ships rose on the wind,
And the sun, sinking low, on the serried shields shined,
    In the years that are fled.

"Pevensey!" The shout from a thousand ships rung;
To Hastings we marched the green hill-sides among,
And there the great war-song of Roland we sung,
    In the years that are fled.

And calm was the evening, the moon it was round,
The dead and the dying lay thick on the ground,
As I stood by the side of young Harold discrowned,
    In the years that are fled.

My army from slumber awakened each day
The yeomen to harry, the foemen to slay;
They fought by the Humber, they fought by the Tay,
> In the years that are fled.

Fécamp glows before me, — the feasts debonair, ‧
The troubadours' dance in the torch-lighted air,
The full wine that flowed 'neath the coronals there,
> In the years that are fled.

The scutcheon of Conqueror shines on the wall;
My triumphs are arrased in yonder gold hall,
And chronicled there, where the tapestries fall,
> Are the years that are fled.

My red wars are ending; o'er wrinkles of care
Time's coronet silver encircles my hair;
Alas and alas for the son of Robèrt,
> And the years that are fled.

Hark! . . . A young mother sings on the terrace below
To the babe on her breast an old rune of Bayeux;
My crown would I give its sweet slumbers to know,
> And to lie in its stead!

I long for my youth, for the heart of a friend,
For the peace that the palms of the Crucified send.
My conquests are dust, and darkens the end,
> The years that are dead.

[Originally published in the *Atlantic Monthly.*

II.

CHAMPLAIN.

QUEBEC, 1635.

'TIS the Fortress of St. Louis,
 The Church of Recoverance ;
And hang o'er the crystal Crosses
 The silver Lilies of France.
In the fortress a knight lies dying,
 · In the church are priests at prayer,
And the bell of the Angelus sweetly
 Throbs out on the crimsoned air.

The noblest knight is dying
 That ever served a king ;
And he looks from the fortress window
 As the bells of the Angelus ring.
Old scenes come back to his vision ;
 Again his ship's canvases swell
In the harbor of gray St. Malo,
 In the haven of fair Rochelle.
He sees the imparadised ocean
 That he dared when his years were young ;
The lagoons where his lateen-sail drifted
 As the Southern Cross over it hung ;
Acadie ; the Richelieu's waters ;
 The lakes through the midlands that rolled ;
And the Cross that he planted wherever
 He lifted the Lilies of gold.

He lists to the Angelus ringing,
　He folds his thin hands on his breast,
And, lo, o'er the pine clouded forests
　A Star verges low in the West:

I.

Star on the bosom of the West —
　Chime on, O bell, chime on, O bell ! —
To-night, with visions I am blest,
　And filled with light ineffable !
No angels sing in crystal air,
　No clouds 'neath seraph's footsteps glow,
No feet of seers, o'er mountains fair,
　A portent follows far, but lo !
　　A Star is glowing in the West,
　　　The world shall follow it from far,
　　Chime on, O Christmas bells, chime on,
　　Shine on, shine on, O Western Star !

II.

In yonder church that storms have iced —
　I founded it upon this rock —
I've daily kissed the feet of Christ,
　In worship with my little flock.
But I am dying — I depart.
　Like Simeon old my glad feet go.
A star is shining in my heart,
　Such as the Magi saw, and lo,
　　A Star is shining in the West,
　　　The world shall hail it from afar,
　　Chime on, O Christmas bells, chime on !
　　Shine on, shine on, O Western Star !

III.

Beside the Fleur de Lis of France,
   The faith I've planted in the North ;
Ye messengers of Heaven, advance,
   Ye mysteries of the Cross, shine forth !
I know the value of the earth ;
   I've learned its lessons ; it is done ;
One soul alone outweighs in worth
   The fairest kingdom of the sun.*
     Star on the bosom of the West,
      My dim eyes follow thee afar ;
     Chime on, chime on, O Christmas bells !
     Shine on, shine on, O golden Star !

IV.

In dreams St. Malo's port I see,
   The havens fair of old Rochelle,
My lateen-sails again flow free,
   And in the seas of crystal swell.
O Richelieu, O Richelieu,
   For thee I sought these regions broad,
And to the Lilies I've been true ;
   My prince, these kingdoms are for God.
     Star on the bosom of the West,
      My soul doth follow thee afar ;
     Chime on, chime on, O Christmas bells !
     Shine on, shine on, O golden Star !

V.

Hark ! music fills my dying ear,
   " Immanuel ! " They sing His name,

* Champlain's letters to Richelieu.

As though again to earth drew near
  Celestial messengers of flame.
The priest stands on the altar stairs,
  And swings the incense cup of gold,
The midnight mass is said, and prayers,
  Hark! 'tis the midnight anthem old —
The hymn I sung upon the sea,
  Beneath Selene's golden car
That fills the air with melody —
  Shine on, shine on, O golden Star!

VI.

What rapture! hear the sweet choir sing,
  While death's cold shadows o'er me fall,
Beneath the Lilies of my king;
  Go, light the lamps in yonder hall.
Mine eyes have seen the Christ-Star glow
  Above the New World's temple gates.
Go forth, celestial heralds, go,
  Earth's fairest empire thee awaits!
    Star on the bosom of the West,
      What feet shall follow thee from far?
    Chime on, O Christmas bells, chime on!
      Shine on, forever, golden Star!

'Twas Christmas morn; the sun arose
  'Mid clouds o'er the St. Lawrence broad,
And fell a sprinkling of the snows
  As from the uplifted hand of God.
Dead in the fortress lay the knight,
  His white hands crossed upon his breast —

Dead, he whose clear prophetic sight
  Beheld the Christ-Star in the West.
That morning, 'mid the turrets white,
  The low flag told the empire's loss;
They hung the Lilies o'er the knight,
  And by the Lilies set the Cross.

Long on Quebec's immortal heights
  Has Champlain slept, the knight of God.
The Western Star shines on, and lights
  The growing empires, fair and broad.
And though are gone the knights of France,
  Still lives the spirit of the North;
The heralds of the Star advance,
  And Truth's eternal light shines forth.

[Originally published in *Youth's Companion.*

THE CLOCKS OF KENILWORTH.

SUGGESTED BY THE RUINED CHURCH AT JAMESTOWN,
VIRGINIA.

" The clocks were stopped at the banquet-hour."

AN ivy spray in my hand I hold,
The kindly ivy that covers the mould
Of ruined halls ; it was brought to me
From Kenilworth Castle, over the sea —
O, Ivy, Ivy, I think of that Queen,
Who once swept on her way through the oak walls
    green,
To Kenilworth, far in the gathering glooms,
Her cavalcade white with silver plumes.
   They are gone, all gone, those knights of old,
   With their red-cross banners and spurs of gold,
   And thou dost cover their castle's mould,
     O, Ivy, Ivy, dark and cold !

O, Ivy, Ivy — I see that hour.
The great bell strikes in the signal-tower,
The banners lift in the ghostly moon,
The bards Provençal their harps attune,
The fiery fountains play on the lawns,
The glare of the rocket startles the fawns,
The trumpets peal, and roll the drums,
And the Castle thunders, " She comes, she comes ! "

They are gone, all gone, those knights of old,
 With their red-cross banners and spurs of gold,
 And thou dost cover their castle's mould,
   O, Ivy, Ivy, dark and cold!

But hark! the notes of the culverin!
To the Castle's portal, trooping in,
A thousand courtiers torches bear,
And the turrets flame in the dusty air.
The Castle is ringing, " All hail! all hail! "
Ride slowly, O Queen! 'mid the walls of mail,
And now let the courtliest knight of all
Lead thy jewelled feet to the banquet hall ;
A thousand goblets await thee there,
And the great clocks lift their faces in air.
   They are gone, all gone, those knights of old,
    With their red-cross banners and spurs of gold,
    And thou dost cover their castle's mould,
      O, Ivy, Ivy, dark and cold!

O, Ivy true ; O, Ivy old,
The great clocks stare on the cups of gold
Like dreadful eyes, and their hands pass on
The festive minutes, one by one.
— " Dying — dying," they seem to say —
" This too — this too — shall pass away,"
And the knights look up, and the knights look down,
And their fair white brows on the great clocks frown.
   They are gone, all gone, those knights of old,
    With their red-cross banners and spurs of gold,

And thou dost cover their castle's mould,
  O, Ivy, Ivy, dark and cold!

On the dais the Queen now stands — and falls
A silence deep on the blazing halls;
She opes her lips — but, hark! now dare
The clocks to beat in the stillness there?
— "Dying — dying," they seem to say —
"This too — this too — shall pass away!"
And the Queen looks up, and with stony stare
The high clocks look on the proud Queen there.
  They are gone, all gone, those knights of old,
  With their red-cross banners and spurs of gold,
  And thou dost cover their castle's mould,
    O, Ivy, Ivy, dark and cold!

Then the dark knights say, "What is wanting here?"
"That the hour should last" — so said a peer.
"The hour *shall* last!" the proud earl calls;
"Ho! Stop the clocks in the banquet halls!"
And the clocks' slow pulses of death were stilled,
And the gay earl smiled, and the wine was spilled,
And the jewelled Queen at the dumb clocks laughed,
And the flashing goblet raised and quaffed.
  They are gone, all gone, those knights of old,
  With their red-cross banners and spurs of gold,
  And thou dost cover their castle's mould,
    O, Ivy, Ivy, dark and cold!

But time went on, though the clocks were dead;
O'er the dewy oaks rose the morning red.

The earl of that sun-crowned castle died,
And never won the Queen for his bride,
And the Queen grew old, and withered, and gray,
And at last in her halls of state she lay
On her silken cushions, bejewelled, but poor,
And the courtiers listened without the door.
  They are gone, all gone, those knights of old,
    With their red-cross banners and spurs of gold,
    And thou dost cover their castle's mould,
      O, Ivy, Ivy, dark and cold!

The twilight flushes the arrased hall,
The Night comes still, and her velvet pall
Of diamonds cold drops from her hand,
And still as the stars is the star-lit land.
Men move like ghosts through the castle's rooms,
But the old clocks talk 'mid the regal glooms:
— " Dying — dying," they seem to say,
Till the astrals pale in the light of day.
  They are gone, all gone, those knights of old,
    With their red-cross banners and spurs of gold,
    And thou dost cover their castle's mould,
      O, Ivy, Ivy, dark and cold!

O, Ivy true, as they listen there,
On the helpless Queen the great clocks stare,
And over and over again they say,
" This too — this too — shall pass away."
And she clasps the air with her fingers old,
And the hall is shadowy, empty, and cold.

" Life ! life ! " she cries, "my all would I give
For a moment, one moment, O, Time, to live ! "
  They are gone, all gone, those knights of old,
  With their red-cross banners and spurs of gold,
  And thou dost cover their castle's mould,
    O, Ivy, Ivy, dark and cold !

On her crownless brow fell white her hair
And she buried her face in her cushions there :
"One moment ! " — it echoed through the hall,
But the clock stopped not on the arrased wall.
—— There is a palace whose dial towers
Uplift no record of vanishing hours,
Disease comes not to its doors, nor falls
Death's dusty steps in its golden halls.
  And more than crowns, or castles old,
  Or red-cross banners, or spurs of gold,
  That palace key it is to hold,
    O, Ivy, Ivy, dark and cold !

[Originally published in *Wide Awake.*

LIBERATORS.

I.

LINCOLN'S LAST DREAM.

[President Lincoln, just before the assassination, is said to have remarked to Mrs. Lincoln, "When my cares of State are over, I wish to go to Palestine."]

I.

APRIL flowers were in the hollows; in the air were
    April bells,
And the wings of purple swallows rested on the battle
    shells.
From the war's long scene of horror now the nation
    found release;
All the day the old war bugles blew the blessed notes
    of peace.
      'Thwart the twilight's damask curtains
        Fell the night upon the land,
      Like God's smile of benediction
        Shadowed faintly by his hand.
In the twilight, in the dusklight, in the starlight, every-
    where,
Banners waved like gardened flowers in the palpitating
    air.

II.

In Art's temple there were greetings, gentle hurryings
    of feet,
And triumphant strains of music rose amid the num-
    bers sweet.

Soldiers gathered, heroes gathered, women beautiful
    were there :
Will *he* come, the land's Beloved, there to rest an hour
    from care ?
      Will he come who for the people
        Long the cross of pain has borne, —
      Prayed in silence, wept in silence,
        Held the hand of God alone ?
Will he share the hour of triumph, now his mighty work
    is done ?
Here receive the people's plaudits, now the victory is
    won ?

III.

O'er thy dimpled waves, Potomac, softly now the moon-
    beams creep ;
O'er far Arlington's green meadows, where the brave
    forever sleep.
'Tis Good Friday ; bells are tolling, bells of chapels
    beat the air
On thy quiet shores, Potomac ; Arlington, serene and
    fair.
      And he comes, the nation's hero,
        From the White House, worn with care ;
      Hears the name of " Lincoln ! " ringing
        In the thronged streets, everywhere ;
Hears the bells, — what memories bringing to his long-
    uplifted heart !
Hears the plaudits of the people as he gains the Hall
    of Art.

IV.

Throbs the air with thrilling music, gayiy onward sweeps
    the play;
But he little heeds the laughter, for his thoughts are
    far away;
And he whispers faintly, sadly, " Oft a blessed Form
    I see,
Walking calmly 'mid the people on the shores of
    Galilee;
        Oft I've wished His steps to follow.
          Follow Him, the Man Divine;
        When the cares of State are over,
          I will go to Palestine,
And the paths the Blessed followed I will walk from
    sea to sea,
Follow Him who healed the people on the shores of
    Galilee."

V.

Hung the flag triumphant o'er him; and his eyes with
    tears were dim,
Though a thousand eyes before him lifted oft their
    smiles to him.
Forms of statesmen, forms of heroes, women beautiful
    were there,
But it was another vision that had calmed his brow of
    care:
        Tabor glowed in light before him,
          Carmel in the evening sun;
        Faith's strong armies grandly marching
          Through the vale of Esdralon;

Bethany's palm-shaded gardens, where the Lord the
    sisters met,
And the Pascal moon arising o'er the brow of Olivet.

VI.

Now the breath of light applauses rose the templed
    arches through,
Stirred the folds of silken banners, mingled red and
    white and blue ;
But the Dreamer seemed to heed not : rose the past his
    eye before, —
Armies guarding the Potomac, flashing through the
    Shenandoah ;
        Gathering armies, darkening navies,
           Heroes marching forth to die ;
        Chickamauga, Chattanooga,
           And the Battle of the Sky ;
Silent prayers to free the bondmen in the ordeal of fire,
And God's angel's sword uplifted to fulfil his heart's
    desire.

VII.

Thought he of the streets of Richmond on the late
    triumphant day
When the swords of vanquished leaders at his feet sur-
    rendered lay ;
When, amid the sweet bells ringing, all the sable multi-
    tudes
Shouted forth the name of "Lincoln !" like a rushing
    of the floods ;

Thought of all his heart had suffered ;
　　All his struggles and renown ;
　　Dreaming not that just above him
　　Lifted was the martyr's crown ;
Seeing not the dark form stealing through the music-
　　haunted air ;
Knowing not that 'mid the triumph the betrayer's feet
　　were there.

VIII.

Flash ! what scymetar of fire lit the flag with lurid light ?
Hush ! what means that shuddering silence, what that
　　woman's shriek of fright ?
Puff of smoke ? the call bell ringing ? why has stopped
　　the airy play ?
Why the fixed looks of the players that a moment
　　passed were light and gay ?
　　　　Why the murmurings, strange, uncertain,
　　　　　Why do faces turn so white,
　　　　Why descends the affrighted curtain
　　　　　Like a wild cloud 'thwart the sight ?
Why the brute cries ? why the tumult ? Has Death
　　found the hall of art ?
Hush !　What say those quivering whispers turning into
　　stone each heart ?

IX.

April morning ; flags are blowing ; 'thwart each flag a
　　sable bar.
Dead, the leader of the people ; dead, the world's great
　　commoner.

Bells on the Potomac tolling ; tolling by the Sangamon ;
Tolling from the broad Atlantic to the Ocean of the Sun.
        Friend and foe clasp hands in silence,
            Listen to the low prayers said,
        Hear the people's benedictions,
            Hear the nations praise the dead.
Lovely land of Palestina ! he thy shores will never see,
But, his dream fulfilled, he follows Him who walked in
    Galilee.

II

ALEXANDER.

ON THE NIGHT BEFORE THE RUSSIAN EMANCIPATION.

I.

It was midnight on the Finland,
    And, o'er the wastes of snow,
From the crystal sky of Winter
    The lamps of God hung low.
A sea of ice was the Neva,
    In the white light of the stars,
And it locked its arms in silence
    Round the city of the Tzars.

II.

The palace was mantled in shadow,
    And, dark in the starlit space,
The monolith rose before it
    From its battle-trophied base.

And the cross that crowned the column
　　Seemed reaching to the stars,
O'er the white streets, wrapped in silence,
　　Round the palace of the Tzars.

III.

The chapel's mullioned windows
　　Are flushed with a sudden light ;
Who comes to the shadowy altar
　　In the stillness of the night ?
What prince with a deep heart burden
　　Approaches the jewelled shrine,
And looks from the silver chalice
　　To the arm of Power Divine ?

IV.

In that still church, strains celestial
　　Like Bethlehem's fill his ears,
And the mystic words " Good tidings "
　　And " Peace on Earth " he hears.
The priests hear not the voices
　　As the golden lamps low swing : —
But who is the muffled stranger,
　　In whose prayers the angels sing ?

V.

'Tis the Tzar, whose word in the morning
　　Shall make the Russias free
From the Neva to the Ural,
　　From the Steppe to the winter sea ;

Who speaks, and a thousand steeples
    Ring freedom to every man —
From the serf on the white Ladoga
    To the fisher of Astrachan.

VI.

Slept the serf on the Neva and Volga,
    Slept the fisher of Astrachan,
Nor dreamed of that prayer that was lifted
    To God for the manhood of man ;
Of the Tzar at that lone, dim altar,
    At the midnight hour bowed down,
With cross laid heavy upon him,
    While darkness hid the crown.

VII.

The morn set its jewels of rubies
    In the snows of the turret and spire,
And shone the far sea of the Finland,
    A sea of glass mingled with fire.
The Old Guard encircled the palace
    With questioning look on each cheek,
And waited the word that the ukase
    To the zone-girded empire should speak.

VIII.

The voice of the Russias has spoken ;
    Each serf in the Russias is free.
Ring, bells, on the Neva and Volga,
    Ring, bells, on the Caspian Sea.

The triumphs of Peace, Alexander,
  Outshine all thy triumphs of war,
And thou at God's altar wert grander
  Than throned as the conquering Tzar.

IX.

Long, O long, sweet bells of the Russias
  Your voice on the March air fling,
Ring, bells, on the Dwina and Volga.
  Ring, bells, on the Caspian, ring !
O, grand is the prayer of silence
  That ascends from the heart bowed down,
For the soul that life's great cross misses
  Shall miss in all ages its crown.

[Originally published in *Christian Union*.

WHITMAN'S RIDE FOR OREGON.

I.

"An empire to be lost or won!"
  And who four thousand miles will ride
  And climb to heaven the Great Divide,
And find the way to Washington,
    Through mountain cañons, winter snows,
    O'er streams where free the north wind blows?
Who, who will ride from Walla-Walla,
    Four thousand miles, for Oregon?

II.

"An empire to be lost or won?
  In youth to man I gave my all,
  And nought is yonder mountain wall;
If but the will of Heaven be done,
    It is not mine to live or die,
    Or count the mountains low or high,
Or count the miles from Walla-Walla.
    I, I will ride for Oregon.

III.

"An empire to be lost or won?
  Bring me my Cayuse pony then,
  And I will thread old ways again,
Beneath the gray skies' crystal sun.

'Twas on those altars of the air
    I raised the flag, and saw below
    The measureless Columbia flow ;
The Bible oped, and bowed in prayer,
And gave myself to God anew,
And felt my spirit newly born ;
And to my mission I'll be true,
And from the vale of Walla-Walla,
    I'll ride again for Oregon.

IV.

"I'm not my own, myself I've given,
    To bear to savage hordes the word ;
If on the altars of the heaven
    I'm called to die, it is the Lord.
The herald may not wait or choose,
    'Tis his the summons to obey ;
To do his best, or gain or lose,
    To seek the Guide and not the way.
He must not miss the cross, and I
    Have ceased to think of life or death ;
My ark I've builded — Heaven is nigh,
    And earth is but a morning's breath ;
Go, then, my Cayuse pony, bring
    The hopes that seek myself are gone,
And from the vale of Walla-Walla,
    I'll ride again for Oregon."

V.

He disappeared, as not his own,
    He heard the warning ice winds sigh ;
The smoky sun flames o'er him shone,
    On whitened altars of the sky,

As up the mountain sides he rose ;
    The wandering eagle round him wheeled,
The partridge fled, the gentle roes,
    And oft his Cayuse pony reeled
Upon some dizzy crag and gazed
    Down cloudy chasms, falling storms,
While higher yet the peaks upraised
    Against the winds their giant forms.
On, on and on, past Idaho,
    On past the mighty Saline sea,
His covering at night the snow,
    His only sentinel a tree.
On, past Portneuf's basaltic heights,
    On where the San Juan mountains lay,
Through sunless days and starless nights,
    Towards Toas and far Sante Fé.
O'er table-lands of sleet and hail,
    Through pine-roofed gorges, cañons cold,
Now fording streams incased in mail
    Of ice, like Alpine knights of old,
Still on, and on, forgetful on,
    Till far behind lay Walla-Walla,
And far the fields of Oregon.

VI.

The winter deepened, sharper grew
    The hail and sleet, the frost and snow,
Not e'en the eagle o'er him flew,
    And scarce the partridge's wing below.

The land became a long white sea,
  And then a deep with scarce a coast,
The stars refused their light, till he
  Was in the wildering mazes lost.
He dropped rein, his stiffened hand
  Was like a statue's hand of clay,
" My trusty beast, 'tis the command,
  Go on, I leave to thee the way.
I must go on, I must go on,
  Whatever lot may fall to me,
On, 'tis for others' sake I ride,
  For others I may never see,
And dare thy clouds, O Great Divide,
  Not for myself, O Walla-Walla,
Not for myself, O Washington,
But for thy future, Oregon."

VII.

And on and on the dumb beast pressed
  Uncertain, and without a guide,
And found the mountain's curves of rest
  And sheltered ways of the Divide.
His feet grew firm, he found the way
  With storm-beat limbs and frozen breath,
As keen his instincts to obey
  As was his master's eye of faith,
Still on and on, still on and on,
  And far and far grew Walla-Walla,
And far the fields of Oregon.

VIII.

That spring, a man with frozen feet
   Came to the marble halls of State,
And told his mission but to meet
   The chill of scorn, the scoff of hate.
" Is Oregon worth saving?" asked
   The treaty-makers from the coast,
And him, the church with questions tasked,
   And said, "Why did you leave your post?"
Was it for this that he had braved
   The warring storms of mount and sky?
Yes! — yet that empire he had saved,
   And to his post went back to die,
Went back to die for others' sake,
   Went back to die from Washington,
Went back to die for Walla-Walla,
   For Idaho and Oregon.

IX.

At fair Walla-Walla one may see
   The city of the Western North,
And near it graves unmarked there be
   That cover souls of royal worth,
The flag waves o'er them in the sky
   Beneath whose stars are cities born,
And round them mountain-castled lie
   The hundred states of Oregon.

CAMEOS OF AMERICAN HISTORY.

COLUMBUS.

[" God made me the messenger of the new heavens and new earth, and told me where to find them. Reason, charts, and mathematical knowledge had nothing to do with case."— *Columbus.*]

HERE, 'mid these paradises of the seas,
  The roof beneath of this cathedral old,
That lifts its suppliant arms above the trees,
  Each clasping in its hand a cross of gold,
  Columbus sleeps — his crumbling tomb behold!
By faith his soul rose eagle-winged and free,
  And reached that Power whose wisdom never fails,
Walked 'mid the kindred stars, and reverently
  The light earth weighed in God's own golden scales.
A man of passions like to men's was he.
  He overcame them, and with hope and trust
Made strong his soul for highest destiny,
And, following Christ, he walked upon the sea:
  The waves upheld him — what is here is dust.
                                        [At Havana.

ISABELLA.

There was weeping in Granada on that eventful day,
One king in triumph entered in, one vanquished rode
    away,
Down from the Alhambra's minarets was every cres-
    cent flung,
And the cry of "Santiago!" through the jewelled pal-
    ace rung.
    And singing, singing, singing,
    Were the nightingales of Spain.
    But the Moorish monarch, lonely,
    The cadences heard only.
    "They sadly sing," said he,
    "They sadly sing to me,"
    And through the groves melodious
    He rode toward the sea.

There was joy in old Granada, on that eventful day,
One king in triumph entered in, one slowly rode away.
Up the Alcala singing marched the gay cavaliers —
Gained was the Moslem empire of twice three hundred
    years.
    And singing, singing, singing,
    Were the nightingales of Spain.
    But the Moorish monarch, lonely,
    The cadences heard only.

" They sadly sing," said he,
" They sadly sing to me,
   All the birds of Andalusia ! "
   And he rode toward the sea.

Through the groves of Alpuxarrus, on that eventful day,
The vanquished king rode slowly and tearfully away.
He paused upon the Xenil, and saw Granada fair
Wreathed with the sunset's roses in palpitating air.
     And singing, singing, singing,
     Were the nightingales of Spain.
     But the Moorish monarch, lonely,
     The cadences heard only.
   " They sadly sing," said he,
   " They sadly sing to me ;
     Oh, groves of Andalusia ! "
     He rode toward the sea.

The Verga heaped with flowers below the city lay,
And faded in the sunset, as he slowly rode away,
And he paused again a moment amid the cavaliers,
And saw the golden palace shine through the mist of
       tears.
     And singing, singing, singing,
     Were the nightingales of Spain.
     But the Moorish monarch, lonely,
     The cadences heard only.
   " They sadly sing," said he,
   " They sadly sing to me ;
     Farewell, O Andalusia ! "
     And he rode toward the sea.

Past the gardens of Granada rode Isabella fair,
As twilight's parting roses fell on the sea of air;
She heard the lisping fountains, and not the Moslem's
      sighs,
She saw the sun-crowned mountains, and not the tear-
      wet eyes.
    "Sing on," she said, "forever,
      O nightingales of Spain;
      Xenil nor Guadalquivir
      Will *he* ne'er see again.
      Ye sweetly sing," said she,
    "Ye sweetly sing to me."
      She rode toward the palace,
      He rode toward the sea.

"I see above yon palace, your pinnacles of gems
The banners of the chalice, the dual diadems;
It fills my heart with rapture, as from a smile divine,
I feel the will to bless it, if all the world were mine.
    Sing on," she said, "forever,
      O nightingales of Spain;
      Xenil nor Guadalquivir
      Will he ne'er see again.
      Ye sweetly sing," said she,
    "Ye sweetly sing to me."
      She rode toward the capital,
      He rode toward the sea.

THE BIRD THAT SANG TO COLUMBUS.

I.

" PADRE,
As on we go
Into the unknown sea,
The morning splendors rise and glow,
In new horizons still. — Padre, you know,
They said in old Seville 'twould not be so;
They said black deeps and flaming air
Were ocean's narrow bound;
Light everywhere
We've found,

Padre.

II.

" Behold !
The fronded palms
That fan the earth, and hold
Aloft their mellowed fruit in dusky arms
Above these paradises of the sea.
Hark! hear the birds. — A land bird sang to me
Upon the mast on that mysterious morn
Before the new world rose :
Sang, and was gone,
Who knows,

Padre ?

III.

"But he,
That joyful bird,
Was sent by Heaven to me
To sing the sweetest song man ever heard!
He came amid the mutiny and strife,
And sang his song in these new airs of life ;
Sang of the Edens of those glorious seas,
Then westward made his flight,
On the land breeze,
From sight,

Padre."

VERAZZANO.

AT RHODES AND RHODE ISLAND.[*]

In the tides of the warm south wind it lay,
  And its grapes turned wine in the fires of noon,
And its roses blossomed from May to May,
  And their fragrance lingered from June to June.

There dwelt old heroes at Ilium famed,
  There, bards reclusive, of olden odes;
And so fair were the fields of roses, they named
  The bright sea-garden the Isle of Rhodes.

Fair temples graced each blossoming field,
  And columned halls in gems arrayed;
Night shaded the sea with her jewelled shield,
  And sweet the lyres of Orpheus played.

The Helios spanned the sea: its flame
  Drew hither the ships of Pelion's pines,
And twice a thousand statues of fame
  Stood mute in twice a thousand shrines.

[*] The legend is that Verazzano gave the name to Rhode Island from the Island of Rhodes, or Roses, in the Mediterranean.

And her mariners went, and her mariners came,
  And sang on the seas the olden odes,
And at night they remembered the Helios' flame,
  And at morn the sweet fields of the roses of Rhodes.

From the palm land's shades to the lands of pines,
  A Florentine crossed the Western sea ;
He sought new lands and golden mines,
  And he sailed 'neath the flag of the *Fleur de lis.*

He saw at last, in the sunset's gold,
  A wonderful island so fair to view
That it seemed like the Island of Roses old
  That his eyes in his wondering boyhood knew.

'Twas summer time, and the glad birds sung
  In the hush of noon in the solitudes ;
From the oak's broad arms the green vines hung ;
  Sweet odors blew from the resinous woods.

He rounded the shores of the summer sea,
  And he said as his feet the white sands pressed,
And he planted the flag of the *Fleur de lis :*
  " I have come to the Island of Rhodes in the West.

" While the mariners go, and the mariners come,
  And sing on lone waters the olden odes
Of the Grecian seas and the ports of Rome,
  They ever will think of the roses of Rhodes."

To the isle of the West he gave the name
  Of the isle he had loved in the Grecian sea ;
And the Florentine went away as he came,
  'Neath the silver flag of the *Fleur de lis.*

O fair Rhode Island, thy guest was true,
   He felt the spirit of beauteous things;
Thy sea-wet roses were faint and few,
   But memory made them the gardens of kings.

The Florentine corsair sailed once more,
   Out into the West o'er a rainy sea,
In search of another wonderful shore
   For the crown of France and the *Fleur de lis.*

But returned no more the Florentine brave
   To the courtly knights of fair Rochelle;
'Neath the lilies of France he found a grave,
   And not 'neath the roses he loved so well.

But the lessons of beauty his fond heart bore
   From the gardens of God were never lost;
And the fairest name of the Eastern shore
   Bears the fairest isle of the Western coast.

PONCÉ DE LEON.

I.

A STORY of Poncé de Leon,
  A voyager, withered and old,
Who came to the sunny Antilles,
  In quest of a country of gold.
He was wafted past islands of spices,
  As bright as the Emerald seas,
Where all the forests seem singing,
  So thick were the birds on the trees;
The sea was as clear as the azure,
  And so deep and so pure was the sky
That the jasper-walled city seemed shining
  Just out of the reach of the eye.
By day his light canvas he shifted,
  And rounded strange harbors and bars;
By night, on the full tides he drifted,
  'Neath the low-hanging lamps of the stars.
Near the glimmering gates of the sunset,
  In the twilight empurpled and dim,
The sailors uplifted their voices,
  And sang to the Virgin a hymn.
"Thank the Lord!" said De Leon, the sailor,
  At the close of the rounded refrain;
"Thank the Lord, the Almighty, who blesses
  The ocean-swept banner of Spain!

The shadowy world is behind us,
   The shining Cipango before;
Each morning the sun rises brighter
   On ocean, and island, and shore.
And still shall our spirits grow lighter,
   As prospects more glowing unfold;
Then on, merry men! to Cipango,
   To the West, and the regions of gold!"

II.

There came to De Leon, the sailor,
   Some Indian sages, who told
Of a region so bright that the waters
   Were sprinkled with islands of gold.
And they added: "The leafy Bimini,
   A fair land of grottos and bowers,
Is there; and a wonderful fountain
   Upsprings from its gardens of flowers.
That fountain gives life to the dying,
   And youth to the aged restores;
They flourish in beauty eternal,
   Who set but their foot on its shores!"
Then answered De Leon, the sailor:
   "I am withered, and wrinkled, and old;
I would rather discover that fountain
   Than a country of diamonds and gold."

III.

Away sailed De Leon, the sailor,
   Away with a wonderful glee,
Till the birds were more rare in the azure,
   The dolphins more rare in the sea;

Away from the shady Bahamas,
  Over waters no sailor had seen,
Till again on his wondering vision
  Rose clustering islands of green.
Still onward he sped till the breezes
  Were laden with odors, and lo!
A country embedded with flowers,
  A country with rivers aglow!
More bright than the sunny Antilles,
  More fair than the shady Azores.
" Thank the Lord!" said De Leon, the sailor,
  As feasted his eye on the shores,
" We have come to a region, my brothers,
  More lovely than earth, of a truth;
And here is the life-giving fountain, —
  The beautiful fountain of youth."

IV.

Then landed De Leon, the sailor,
  Unfurled his old banner, and sung;
But he felt very wrinkled and withered,
  All around was so fresh and so young.
The palms, ever verdant, were blooming,
  Their blossoms e'en margined the seas;
O'er the streams of the forests, bright flowers
  Hung deep from the branches of trees.
" 'Tis Easter," exclaimed the old sailor;
  His heart was with rapture aflame;
And he said: " Be the name of this region
  As Florida given to fame.

'Tis a fair, a delectable country,
  More lovely than earth, of a truth ;
I soon shall partake of the fountain, —
  The beautiful fountain of youth ! "

v.

But wandered De Leon, the sailor,
  In search of that fountain in vain ;
No waters were there to restore him
  To freshness and beauty again.
And his anchor he lifted, and murmured,
  As the tears gathered fast in his eye,
" I must leave this fair land of the flowers,
  Go back o'er the ocean, and die."
Then back by the dreary Tortugas,
  And back by the shady Azores,
He was borne on the storm-smitten waters
  To the calm of his own native shores.
And that he grew older and older,
  His footsteps enfeebled gave proof ;
Still he thirsted in dreams for the fountain, —
  The beautiful fountain of youth.

VI.

One day the old sailor lay dying
  On the shores of a tropical isle,
And his heart was enkindled with rapture,
  And his face lighted up with a smile.
He thought of the sunny Antilles,
  He thought of the shady Azores,
He thought of the dreamy Bahamas,
  He thought of fair Florida's shores.

And, when in his mind he passed over
  His wonderful travels of old,
He thought of the heavenly country,
  Of the city of jasper and gold.
"Thank the Lord!" said De Leon, the sailor,
  "Thank the Lord for the light of the truth,
I now am approaching the fountain, —
  The beautiful fountain of youth."

VII.

The cabin was silent: at twilight
  They heard the birds singing a psalm,
And the wind of the ocean low sighing
  Through groves of the orange and palm.
The sailor still lay on his pallet,
  The cool sail spread o'er him a roof,
His soul had gone forth to discover
  The beautiful fountain of youth.

THE LEGEND OF WAUKULLA.

THROUGH darkening pines the cavaliers marched on
    their sunset way,
  While crimson in the trade-winds rolled far Appala-
    chee Bay,
Above the water-levels rose palmetto crowns like ghosts
Of kings primeval; them, behind, the shadowy pines in
    hosts.
      " O cacique, brave and trusty guide,
      Are we not near the spring,
The fountain of eternal youth that health to age doth
    bring?"
      The cacique sighed,
      And Indian guide,
      " The fount is fair,
          Waukulla!

" But vainly to the blossomed flower will come the
    autumn rain,
And never youth's departed days come back to age
    again;
The future in the spirit lies, and earthly life is brief,
'Tis *you* that say the fount hath life," so said the Indian
    chief.

"Nay, Indian king; nay, Indian king,
Thou knowest well the spring,
And thou shalt die if thou dost fail our feet to it to
bring."
The cacique sighed,
And Indian guide,
"The spring is bright,
Waukulla!"

Then said the guide, "O men of Spain, a wondrous
fountain flows
From deep abodes of gods below, and health on men
bestows.
Blue are its deeps and green its walls, and from its
waters gleam
The water-stars, and from it runs the pure Waukulla's
stream.
But men of Spain, but men of Spain,
'Tis *you* who say that spring
Eternal youth and happiness to men again will bring."
The cacique sighed,
And Indian guide,
"The fount is clear,
Waukulla!"

"March on, the land enchanted is; march on, ye men
of Spain;
Who would not taste the bliss of youth and all its hopes
again.
Enchanted is the land; behold! enchanted is the air;
The very heaven is domed with gold; there's beauty
everywhere!"

So said De Leon. " Cavaliers,
  We're marching to the spring,
The fountain of eternal youth, that health to age will
    bring ! "
        The cacique sighed,
        And Indian guide,
        " The fount is pure,
            Waukulla ! "

Beneath the pines, beneath the yews, the deep magnolia
  shades,
The clear Waukulla swift pursues its way through floral
  glades ;
Beneath the pines, beneath the yews, beneath night's
  falling shade,
Beneath the low and dusky moon still marched the
  cavalcade.
      " The river widens," said the men ;
      " Are we not near the spring,
The fountain of eternal youth that health to age doth
  bring ? "
        The cacique sighed,
        And Indian guide,
        " The spring is near,
            Waukulla !

" The fount is fair and bright and clear, and pure its
  waters run ;
Waukulla, lovely in the moon and beauteous in the sun.
But vainly to the blossomed flower will come the autumn
  rain,
And never youth's departed days come back to man again.

O men of Spain! O men of Spain!
'Tis you that say the spring
Eternal youth and happiness to withered years will
    bring!"
        The cacique sighed,
        And Indian guide,
        "The fount is deep,
            Waukulla!"

The river to a grotto led, as to a god's abode;
There lay the fountain bright with stars; stars in its
    waters flowed;
The mighty live-oaks round it rose, in ancient mosses
    clad;
De Leon's heart beat high for joy; the cavaliers were
    glad,
        "O men of Spain! O men of Spain,
        This surely is the spring,
The fountain fair that health and joy to faces old doth
    bring!"
        The cacique sighed.
        And Indian guide,
        "The spring is old,
            Waukulla!"

"Avalla, O my trusty friend that we this day should
    see!
Strip off thy doublet and descend the glowing fount
    with me!"
"The saints! I will," Avalla said. "Already young
    I feel,
And younger than my sons shall I return to old Castile."

Then plunged De Leon in the spring
And then Avalla old,
Then slowly rose each wrinkled face above the waters
cold.
 The cacique sighed,
 And Indian guide,
 " The fount is false,
  Waukulla ! "

O vainly to the blossomed flower will come the autumn
rain,
And never youth's departed days come back to man
again ;
The crowns Castilian could not bring the withered stalk
a leaf,
But came a sabre flash that morn, and fell the Indian
chief.
 Another sabre flash, and then
 The guide beside him lay,
And red the clear Waukulla ran toward Appalachee Bay,
 Then from the dead
 The Spaniards fled,
 And curse the spring,
  Waukulla.

" Like comrades life was left behind, the years shall o'er
me roll,
For all the hope that man can find lies hidden in the soul.
Ye white sails lift, and drift again across the southern
main ;
There wait for me, there wait us all, the hollow tombs
of Spain ! "

Beneath the liquid stars the sails
Arose and went their way,
And bore the gray-haired cavaliers from Appalachee
Bay.
The young chief slept,
And maiden wept,
Beside the bright
Waukulla.

[Originally published in *New England Journal of Education.*

DE SOTO.

TAMPA.

AND this is Tampa : yonder lies the Bay
    That Spanish cavaliers
Enchanted saw upon their unknown way,
    In far and faded years, —

That to their eyes so calm and placid seemed,
    So bright and wondrous fair,
They drifted on with silent lips, and dreamed
    The Holy Ghost was there.

Here lies a fortress old, a field of death ;
    And here, as years increase,
The useless cannon hide their heads beneath
    The snow-white sands of peace.

The Gulf winds warm the orange orchards stir,
    And from dark trees like walls,
In long festoons and threads of gossamer,
    The trailing gray moss falls.

And ships come in from tropic seas, and go,
    And sails the Gulf winds fan ;
And few do know, or seem to care to know,
    That here that march began

That set that crown of empires in the West,
  And gave the nations birth
That stand like gracious queens, above the rest,
  Upon the thrones of earth.

The town is fair, and fairer yet the Bay,
  And warm the trade-winds blow
Where lateen-sails moved on their lonely way,
  Three centuries ago.

De Soto's hands lie deep beneath the wave,
  Dust are his cavaliers ;
The cypressed waters murmuring o'er his grave,
  The silent pilot hears

In that far river where they laid him down,
  Where low the ring-doves sigh,
And oft the full moon drops her silver crown,
  From night's meridian sky.

And here, where first his banners caught the breeze,
  The peopled towns arise ; ·
And his great faith, that piloted the seas
  Beneath uncertain skies,

And dared the wilds by Christian feet untrod,
  Is strong with hope to man ;
And here, where touched the new world's ark of God,
  Fair skies the rainbows span.

O Tampa, Tampa, near the Gulf's warm tide !
  Who would not linger here,
Where, on the homes the orange-gardens hide,
  June smileth all the year?

Where never comes the autumn nor the spring,
  Nor summer's fiercer glow ;
Where never cease the mocking-birds to sing,
  Nor roses new to blow.

                [Tampa, Florida.

IN TAMPA BAY.

TAMPA BAY.

{Named by De Soto, on Ash Wednesday, " Santo Esperitu."}

A PULSELESS sea of summers never ending,
    Where suns eternal shine,
And clouds, like priests the altar steps ascending,
    Baptisms bring divine —
        " Santo Esperitu."

While half the sky a roof of gold is shining,
    And curtaining clouds hang low,
The distant pines the far horizons lining,
    Burn in the afterglow —
        " Santo Esperitu."

The white sails dip as in a world of dreaming,
    Then right and slowly drift,
And clouds of ibis, in the red light gleaming,
    Their silver wings uplift —
        " Santo Esperitu."

The sun is liquid in the morn and even,
    An altar flame at noon,
And like the shadow of the gate of heaven
    Falls on the sea the moon —
        " Santo Esperitu."

The Spanish voyager thrilled as on he drifted,
    Past shores of ghostly woods,
O'er which, like crowns, the airy palms seemed lifted,
    O'er floral seas and floods —
        "Santo Esperitu."

The vision raised his soul devout toward heaven,
    Parted his lips ; what name
Should be to such a placid sun sea given,
    And breathed for aye to fame ? —
        "Santo Esperitu."

The words were spoken ; 'twas well !   O sea, inherit
    The name the voyager gave !
And long recall the light within his spirit
    Who saw God on the wave —
        "Santo Esperitu."

Tampa, Florida.

        [Originally appeared in *Boston Transcript.*

THE FIRE DANCE.

ORTIZ.

[Time of De Soto.]

"Go bring the captive, he shall die,"
  He said, with faltering breath ;
"Him stretch upon a scaffold high,
  And light the fire of death !"
The young Creeks danced the captive round,
  And sang the Song of Doom, —
"Fly, fly, ye hawks, in the open sky,
  Fly, wings of the warrior's plume !"

They brought the fagots for the flame,
  The braves and maids together,
When came the princess —sweet her name :
  The Red Flamingo Feather.
Then danced the Creeks the scaffold round,
  And sang the Song of Doom, —
"Fly, fly, ye hawks, in the open sky,
  Fly, wings of the warrior's plume !"

In shaded plumes of silver gray,
  The young Creeks danced together,
But she danced not with them that day,
  The Red Flamingo Feather.
Wild sped the feet the scaffold round,
  Wild rose the Song of Doom, —
"Fly, fly, ye hawks, in the open sky,
  Fly, wings of the warrior's plume!"

They stretched the stranger from the sea,
  Above the fagots lighted, —
Ortiz, — a courtly man was he,
  With deeds heroic knighted.
And sped the feet the scaffold round,
  And rose the Song of Doom, —
"Fly, fly, ye hawks, in the open sky,
  Fly, wings of the warrior's plume!"

The white smoke rose, the braves were gay,
  The war drums beat together,
But sad in heart and face that day
  Was Red Flamingo Feather.
They streaked with flames the dusky air,
  They shrieked the Song of Doom, —
"Fly, fly, ye hawks, in the open sky,
  Fly, wings of the warrior's plume!"

"Dance, dance, my girl, the torches gleam,
  Dance, dance, the gray plumes gather,
Dance, dance, my girl, the war-hawks scream,
  Dance, Red Flamingo Feather!"

More swiftly now the torches sped,
  Amid the Dance of Doom, —
" Fly, fly, ye hawks, in the open sky,
  Fly, wings of the warrior's plume ! "

She knelt upon the green moss there,
  And clasped her father's knees :
" My heart is weak, O father, spare
  The wanderer from the seas ! "
Like madness now swept on the dance,
  And rose the Song of Doom, —
" Fly, fly, ye hawks, in the open sky,
  Ye wings of the warrior's plume ! "

" Grand were the men who sailed away,
  And he is young and brave ;
'Tis small in heart the weak to slay,
  'Tis great in heart to save."
He saw the torches sweep the air,
  He heard the Song of Doom, —
" Fly, fly, ye hawks, in the open sky,
  Fly, wings of the warrior's plume ! "

" My girl, I know thy heart would spare
  The wanderer from the sea."
" The man is fair, and I am fair,
  And thou art great," said she.
The dance of fire went on and on,
  And on the Song of Doom, —
" Fly, fly, ye hawks, in the open sky,
  Fly, wings of the warrior's plume ! "

The dark chief felt his pride abate :
  "I will the wanderer spare,   ·
My Bird of Peace, since I am great,
  And he, like thee, is fair!"
Then dropped the torches, stopped the dance,
  And died the Song of Doom, —
"Fly, fly, ye hawks, in the open sky,
  Away with the warrior's plume!"

THE FLORIDA IBIS.

The Southern Cross uplifts one glowing star
Between the horizon and the Gulf afar;
I watch the light from the lone river bar,
    And gaze across the sea.

A sea, on which an hundred sunsets flow,
Whose tides around an hundred islands glow,
Where lies the sky above in deeps below, —
    A shadow falls on me.

Has heaven opened? — do evangels fly,
As in the prophet's heaven, across the sky?
An hundred silver wings now fill my eye,
    A cloud of wings, as one.

O Ibis, Ibis! whose thin wings of white
Scarce stir the roses of the sunset light,
When Day dissolving leaves the coasts to Night,
    And far seas hide the sun;

From weedy weirs where blaze the tropic noons,
Savannas dark where cool the fiery moons;
From still Lake Worth, and mossy-walled lagoons,
    Where never footsteps stray;

To far Clear Water, and its isles of pine,
From beryl seas to seas of opaline,
Those level coasts where helpless sea conchs shine,
  Thou driftest on thy way!

O Ibis, Ibis, bird of Hermes bold,
The avatar to men from gates of gold,
That blessed all eyes that saw thy wings of old,
  My thought, like thee, hath wings.

I follow thee, as cool the shadows fall,
And burn the stars on yon horizon's wall;
And Memphian altars, as my thoughts recall,
  My soul to thee upsprings!

My heart to-night with Nature's soul is thrilled,
As with the fire that priests of Isis filled
When rose thy wings, and all the world was stilled
  Beneath thy lucent plumes!

O Ibis, Ibis, whence thy silent flight?
O'er everglades that only fire-flies light,
Magnolias languid with their blooms, when Night
  Gathers from far her glooms.

O'er mossy live-oaks, high palmetto shades,
The cypressed lakelets of the everglades;
O'er rivers dead, and still pines' colonnades,
  Where sweet the jessamine grows;

Where red blooms flame amid the trailing moss,
And streams unnumbered low lianas cross,
Wild orange groves, where in their nests of floss
    The sun-birds find repose.

But hark! what sound upon the stillness breaks?
A rifle shot — a boatman on the lakes,
An Ibis' wing above in silver flakes —
    A white bird downward falls!

O Ibis, Ibis, of the tropic skies,
For whom the arches of the sunsets rise,
God made this world to be thy Paradise,
    Thy Eden without walls.

O Ibis dead, that on the dark lake floats,
Whose dimming eyes see not the sportsmen's boats,
O'er whose torn wing some brutal instinct gloats,
    I wonder if in thee

Live not some spirit, — so the Egyptian thought, —
Some inner life from Life's great Fountain brought,
Something divine from God's great goodness caught,
    Some immortality?

Are all these Paradises dead to thee,
The cool savanna and the purple sea,
The air, thy ocean, where thou wanderest free, —
    I wonder, are they dead?

Or hast thou yet a spirit life, that flies
Like thine own image through the endless skies,
And art thou to some new-born Paradise
    By higher instincts led?

Is death, like life, alike to all that live?
Does God to all a double being give?
Do all that breathe eternal life receive?
    Is thought, where'er it be,

Immortal as the Source from whence it came? —
O living Ibis, in the sunset's flame,
Still flying westward thou and I, the same,
    Can answer not — but *He?*

[Originally published in Youth's Companion.

GALVEZ.

[Who gave the name to Galveston.]

I.

Beneath the dusky tropic stars,
  And misty moons that rose and fled,
His fleet with drooping sails and spars
  Across the breathless Gulf he led, —
    Galvez !
A man of noble mien was he,
Who thought that will was destiny.

II.

In flaming skies he saw afar
  Clear Pensacola's palmy sound,
And, rising o'er the harbor bar,
  The English fortress, turret-crowned, —
    Galvez !
And English flag that claimed the main,
And mocked the double crowns of Spain.

III.

" No ship can ever cross the bar,"
  The pilots, one by one, exclaimed ;
He scanned the glimmering sky afar,
  Where low the red-cross banner flamed, —
    Galvez !
" The ships *shall* cross the bar," said he,
" And plough the white sands like the sea."

IV.

"On, on!"   The unwilling rudders turned
  Toward the narrow channels, when
He in the sinking tides discerned
  The shifting sands, and called again, —
        Galvez!
"Brave men, like gods, events create,
 And will is destiny, — not fate!"

V.

" Back, back again!" broke from the lips
  Of Spanish pilots, old and grave;
Stern grew the master of the ships,
  And grand, as though he ruled the wave, —
        Galvez!
"Bring me the Cross of Spain," said he,
"And launch the life-boat on the sea!"

VI.

The boat was launched; the flag of Spain
  He seized with purpose firm, and then
He leaped upon the level main,
  And proudly turned toward his men, —
        Galvez!
And rowed the life-boat toward the bar,
Then faced the silent crews afar.

VII.

" Shall Spain's sea banner suffer loss?"
  Its folds Castilian rippled down,

Two golden crowns beneath the cross,
    And for a kingdom stood each crown, —
        Galvez !
What sullen eyes beheld him bear
That glimmering banner through the air !

VIII.

Boom ! boom ! The English guns rang clear,
    And fell a shower of leaden rain,
But Galvez heard without a fear,
    And faced the wondering crews of Spain, —
        Galvez !
" Ho, anchors lift ! " loud shouted he,
" And plough the sand-bars like the sea ! "

IX.

Boom ! boom ! the fortress thundered loud,
    And fell again the rain of fire ;
But he, amid his silken cloud,
    Moved on like Arion with his lyre, —
        Galvez !
Moved on, and on, and cried again,
" Ho, follow me, ye ships of Spain ! "

X.

The banner shining on the sea,
    The smoke rolled o'er it like a cloud,
Then from the shade it floated free
    O'er Galvez, still erect and proud,—
        Galvez !
Immortal be his name.
'Tis souls that burn that souls inflame !

XI.

Lo, now the white sails lift on high,
  Gay with the flags of old Castile !
He sees the light ships toward him fly,
  And plough the bar, keel after keel, —
    Galvez !
His soul alone upon the sea
Had won a twofold victory !

XII.

Whene'er I see Galveston's arch
  Above the booming waves, I feel
His spirit still whose mighty march
  The city and the bay reveal, —
    Galvez !
A man of inspiration, he
Who walked with feet of faith the sea.

THE THANKSGIVING IN BOSTON HARBOR.

JULY, 1630.

" PRAISE ye the Lord ! "   The psalm to-day
  Still rises on our ears,
Borne from the hills of Boston Bay
  Through five times fifty years.
When Winthrop's fleet from Yarmouth crept
  Out to the open main,
And through the widening waters swept,
  In April sun and rain.
      " Pray to the Lord with fervent lips," *
      The leader shouted, " Pray " ;
    And prayer arose from all the ships
    As faded Yarmouth Bay.

They passed the Scilly Isles that day,
  And May-days came, and June,
And thrice upon the ocean lay
  The full orb of the moon.
And as that day, on Yarmouth Bay,
  Ere England sunk from view,
While yet the rippling Solent lay
  In April skies of blue,

* " So we came, by the good hand of the Lord, through the
deep comfortably, preaching or expounding the Word of the Lord
every day for ten weeks together."— *Roger Clap*, on the voyage of
the *Mary and John.*

"Pray to the Lord with fervent lips,"
　　Each morn was shouted, "Pray";
And prayer arose from all the ships,
　　As first in Yarmouth Bay.

Blew warm the breeze o'er Western seas,
　　Through Maytime morns, and June,
Till hailed these souls the Isles of Shoals,
　　Low 'neath the summer moon;
And as Cape Ann arose to view,
　　And Norman's Woe they passed,
The wood-doves came the white mists through,
　　And circled round each mast.
　　　　"Pray to the Lord with fervent lips,"
　　　　　　Then called the leader, "Pray";
　　　　And prayer arose from all the ships,
　　　　　　As first in Yarmouth Bay.

Above the sea the hill-tops fair —
　　God's towers — began to rise,
And odors rare breathe through the air,
　　Like balms of Paradise.
Through burning skies the ospreys flew,
　　And near the pine-cooled shores
Danced airy boat and thin canoe,
　　To flash of sunlit oars.
　　　　"Pray to the Lord with fervent lips,"
　　　　　　The leader shouted, "Pray!"
　　　　Then prayer arose, and all the ships
　　　　　　Sailed into Boston Bay.

The white wings folded, anchors down,
  The sea-worn fleet in line,
Fair rose the hills where Boston town
  Should rise from clouds of pine;
Fair was the harbor, summit-walled,
  And placid lay the sea.
" Praise ye the Lord," the leader called;
  " Praise ye the Lord," spake he.
     "Give thanks to God with fervent lips,
     Give thanks to God to-day,"
    The anthem rose from all the ships,
    Safe moored in Boston Bay.

" Praise ye the Lord !" Primeval woods
  First heard the ancient song,
And summer hills and solitudes
  The echoes rolled along.
The Red Cross flag of England blew
  Above the fleet that day,
While Shawmut's triple peaks in view,
  In amber hazes lay.
     " Praise ye the Lord with fervent lips,
     Praise ye the Lord to-day,"
    The anthem rose from all the ships,
    Safe moored in Boston Bay.

The Arabella leads the song —
  The Mayflower sings below —
That erst the Pilgrims bore along
  The Plymouth reefs of snow.

Oh ! never be that psalm forgot,
 That rose o'er Boston Bay,
When Winthrop sung, and Endicott,
 And Saltonstall, that day.
   " Praise ye the Lord with fervent lips,
    Praise ye the Lord to-day ";
   And praise arose from all the ships,
    Like prayers in Yarmouth Bay.

That psalm our fathers sung we sing,
 That psalm of peace and wars,
While o'er our heads unfolds its wing
 The flag of forty stars.
And while the nation finds a tongue
 For nobler gifts to pray,
'Twill ever sing the song they sung
 That first Thanksgiving Day :
   " Praise ye the Lord with fervent lips,
    Praise ye the Lord to-day ";
   So rose the song from all the ships,
    Safe moored in Boston Bay.

Our fathers' prayers have changed to psalms,
 As David's treasures old
Turned, on the Temple's giant arms,
 To lily-work of gold.
Ho ! vanished ships from Yarmouth's tide,
 Ho ! ships of Boston Bay,
Your prayers have crossed the centuries wide
 To this Thanksgiving Day !

We pray to God with fervent lips,
  We praise the Lord to-day,
As prayers arose from Yarmouth ships,
  But psalms from Boston Bay.

[Written for the Thanksgiving dinner of Y. M. C. A., Boston.

ROGER WILLIAMS. *

WHY do I sleep amid the snows,
  Why do the pine boughs cover me,
While dark the wind of winter blows
  Across the Narragansett's sea?

O sense of right! O sense of right,
  Whate'er my lot in life may be,
Thou art to me God's inner light,
  And these tired feet must follow thee.

Yes, still my feet must onward go,
  With nothing for my hope but prayer,
Amid the winds, amid the snow,
  And trust the ravens of the air.

But though alone, and grieved at heart,
  Bereft of human brotherhood,
I trust the whole, and not the part,
  And know that Providence is good.

* " For fourteen weeks he wandered through the dreary forest, sleeping sometimes under a projecting rock or in a hollow tree, living for days together on nuts and dried berries, and sometimes sheltered from the pitiless blast in the smoky cabins of hospitable Indians, and sharing their meagre fare. He had always shown himself friendly to the natives, and had acquired a sufficient knowledge of their language to make known his wants and to converse with them on the great truths of religion."

Self-sacrifice is never lost,
　But bears the seed of its reward;
They who for others leave the most,
　For others gain the most from God.

O sense of right! I must obey,
　And hope and trust, whate'er betide;
I cannot always know my way,
　But I can always know my Guide.

And so for me the winter blows
　Across the Narragansett's sea,
And so I sleep beneath the snows,
　And so the pine boughs cover me.

WILLIAMS AT MOUNT HOPE.

My empty boat rocks in the river weeds shining,
    The Bay lies below me full flowing and free,
I stand on Mount Hope as the day is declining,
    That beautiful summit o'erlooking the sea.

Beyond, the green hills of Pocasset are glowing,
    Afar are the groves of Sowamset ablaze,
And the old Kikemuit below me is flowing
    Through meadowy miles of orchards and maize.

Here once red warriors were wont to assemble
    Here lurid and ghostly their council fires shone,
Here the word of the chief made the ancient tribes
        tremble,
    And the war-whoop rung out from Pometicom's throne.

Gone, gone are the tribes from the scenes that they
        cherished,
    The forests no longer encompass the tide,
The happy flocks sleep where Pometicom perished,
    And wanders the heron where Wetamoo died.

And here on this ocean mound silently lying
    Where tidal waves falling the far seas intone,
Where the sail on the bay like the osprey is flying,
    The olden tribes rest from their warfare unknown.

The mild air of spring-time embeds them in flowers,
   The orioles here from the tropics return,
The grain ripens on them in midsummer hours,
   And mellowing falls by the river sides burn.

Here came the lone exile from Salem aweary,
   By Bigotry hated, lost, homeless and poor,
The outcast of faith, 'mid the snows falling dreary,
   And here to his feet oped the birch palace door.

Here the red hand supplied what a white hand denied
     him,
   Here he wrote in his mind, while the smoke o'er him
     curled,
With the prince at his knee, and the red king beside him,
   The words that unfettered the souls of the world.

Here warmed by the fire of the Indian sages,
   His thoughts o'er the tides of humanity ran,
And the grand parchment formed on whose luminous
     pages
   Was written the law of the birthright of man.

My empty boat rocks in the river weeds shining,
   I leave the sea summit and turn towards the sea,
Yet reluctant I leave, in the day-beams declining,
   These hills where the Lord made humanity free.

SIR HENRY VANE ON THE ISLES OF SCILLY.

I.

IT haunts my days, it haunts my nights,
  It haunts my castle's wall —
No man on earth has any rights
  But those God gives to all.

II.

To me the Scilly Isles are fair,
  A place of happy dreams,
And every cloud that shades the air
  An angel's chariot seems.

III.

What scenes across my vision drift !
  I see the ages blest,
And the Messiah of Nations lift
  Its great gates in the West.

IV.

What though new truths, in light arrayed
  Their treasures new unfold,
And break the Serpent Moses made
  Like him, the seer of old.

V.

Forever while the Light divine
  To noble souls is sweet,
The ark will move, the seraphs shine
  Above the Mercy Seat.

VI.

Whate'er men teach, whate'er believe,
  What may or not be known,
The soul that asks, it shall receive
  The Witness of its own.

VII.

My name the nations fain would blot,
  Since God alone I heed;
My inward evidence comes not
  From state or courtly creed.

VIII.

Now holy night her guardian wing
  Draws slowly o'er the sea;
But in my spirit I can sing
  Of ages grand and free.

IX.

O Thou of life the Source and Cause,
  O Thou of life the End,
All things, by thy eternal laws,
  Towards perfection tend.

X.

Thy purposes I cannot trace
    'Tis mine alone to trust ;
The earth is but a speck in space,
    And human life is dust.

XI.

I know that nothing tends to loss,
    That all things helpful prove,
And all events are tides that cross
    The ocean of thy love.

XII.

Above the rifts of darkness past,
    Fair freedom's star I see ;
Each age is better than the last,
    And shall forever be.

XIII.

This truth divine my spirit feeds,
    I sing amid the calm
As soft the shepherds touched their reeds
    When ceased the angel's psalm.

XIV.

And so the Scilly Isles are fair,
    A place of happy dreams,
And every cloud that shades the air
    An angel's chariot seems.

THE CHURCH OF THE REVOLUTION.

"THE OLD SOUTH STANDS."

LOUD through the still November air
   The clang and clash of fire-bells broke;
From street to street, from square to square,
   Rolled sheets of flame and clouds of smoke
The marble structures reeled and fell,
   The iron pillars bowed like lead;
But one lone spire rang on its bell
    Above the flames.   Men passed, and said,
       " The Old South stands!"

The gold moon, 'gainst a copper sky,
   Hung like a potent in the air,
The midnight came, the wind rose high,
   And men stood speechless in despair.
But, as the marble columns broke,
   And wider grew the chasm red, —
A seething gulf of flame and smoke, —
    The firemen marked the spire and said,
       " The Old South stands!"

Beyond the harbor, calm and fair,
   The sun came up through bars of gold,
Then faded in a wannish glare,
   As flame and smoke still upward rolled.

The princely structures, crowned with art,
  Where Commerce laid her treasures bare ;
The haunts of trade, the common mart,
  All vanished in the withering air, —   .
    " The Old South stands ! "

" The Old South must be levelled soon
  To check the flames and save the street ;
Bring fuse and powder."   But at noon
  The ancient fane still stood complete.
The mitred flame had lipped the spire,
  The smoke its blackness o'er it cast ;
Then, hero-like, men fought the fire,
  And from each lip the watchword passed, —
    " The Old South stands ! "

All night the red sea round it rolled,
  And o'er it fell the fiery rain ;
And, as each hour the old clock told,
  Men said, " 'Twill never strike again ! "
But still the dial-plate at morn
  Was crimsoned in the rising light.
Long may it redden with the dawn,
  And mark the shading hours of night !
    Long may it stand !

Long may it stand ! where help was sought
  In weak and dark and doubtful days ;
Where freedom's lessons first were taught,
  And prayers of faith were turned to praise ;

Where burned the first Shekinah's flame
In God's new temples of the free;
Long may it stand, in freedom's name,
Like Israel's pillar by the sea!
Long may it stand!

AT BENNINGTON.

AUGUST 16, 1777 – 1877.

I.

THE hills are calm, the blue streams flow
    Among the breezy pines,
And over all the pulseless glow
    Of fruiting summer shines.
In bannered air stands yonder town,
    Where freemen rose to stay
The army of the English crown
    An hundred years to-day.

II.

The Walloomscoick purls and croons
    Amid its swampy isles,
And corn-lands dream in fervid noons
    Above its dimpling smiles.
Its boats lay oarless in the sun
    As for the bloody fray
The farmer seized his flintlock gun
    An hundred years to-day.

III.

And peace forsook each hill-side home
    Upon that summer morn,
The daughter left her wheel and loom
    And left the boy the corn.

And when in his accustomed place
  The grandsire knelt to pray,
He buried in his hands his face
  An hundred years to-day.

IV.

The rustic parson met his flock
  Before the morning light ;
" God is our Fortress and our Rock,
  And ours the cause of right.
God's word is ' forward,' cautious Stark,
  Then forward lead the way ! "
The morning rainy rose and dark
  An hundred years to-day.

V.

But broke the cloud, and poured the sun
  Through billowy mists like fire ;
The father marched beside the son,
  The son beside the sire.
Their hearts were strong, their guns were few,
  Before in war array
The red-cross flag of England blew
  An hundred years to-day.

VI.

The fair boy marched beside his sire,
  The sire beside the son,
But in the mellowing evening light
  Returned again but one.

Their graves are here, and calm and still
  The shaded waters stray,
By daisied mounds on many a hill
  Where they repose to-day.

VII.

To-day old Bennington unrolls
  Her flag 'mid summer blooms,
Anew her heroes' names enscrolls
  In legend-haunted homes.
Forever may her blue streams run,
  And west winds o'er them play,
And toss the banners in the sun,
  Forever, as to-day.

THE DEATH OF JEFFERSON.*

"IT IS THE FOURTH?"

I.

'Twas midsummer; cooling breezes all the languid forests fanned,
And the angel of the evening drew her curtain o'er the
land.
Like an isle rose Monticello through the cooled and
rippling trees,
Like an isle in rippling starlight in the silence of the
seas.
Ceased the mocking-bird his singing; said the slaves
with faltering breath,
" 'Tis the Third, and on the morrow Heaven will send
the Angel Death."

II.

In his room at Monticello, lost in dreams the statesman
slept,
Seeing not the still forms round him, seeing not the
eyes that wept,

* July 4, 1826.

Hearing not the old clock ticking in life's final silence
  loud,
Knowing not when night came o'er him like the shadow
  of a cloud.
In the past his soul is living as in fifty years ago,
Hastes again to Philadelphia, hears again the Schuylkill flow —

III.

Meets again the elder Adams — knowing not that far
  away
He is waiting for Death's morrow, on old Massachu-
  setts Bay ;
Meets with Hancock, young and courtly, meets with
  Hopkins, bent and old,
Meets again calm Roger Sherman, fiery Lee, and Car-
  roll bold,
Meets the sturdy form of Franklin, meets the half a
  hundred men
Who have made themselves immortal, — breathes the
  ancient morn again.

IV.

Once again the Declaration in his nerveless hands he
  holds,
And before the waiting statesmen its prophetic hope
  unfolds,
Reads again the words puissant, " All men are created
  free,"
Claims again for man his birthright, claims the world's
  equality,

Hears the coming and the going of an hundred firm-
set feet,
Hears the summer breezes blowing 'mid the oak-trees
cool and sweet,

V.

Sees again tall Patrick Henry by the side of Henry Lee,
Hears him cry, " And will ye sign it ? — it will make all
nations free !
Fear ye not the axe or gibbet ; it shall topple every
throne.
Sign it for the world's redemption ! — All mankind its
truth shall own !
Stars may fall, but truth eternal shall not falter, shall
not fail.
Sign it, and the Declaration shall the voice of ages hail.

VI.

" Sign, and set yon dumb bell ringing, that the people
all may know
Man has found emancipation ; sign, the Almighty wills
it so."
Sees one sign it, then another, till like magic moves
the pen,
Till all have signed it, and it lies there, charter of the
rights of men.*
Hears the small bells, hears the great bell, hanging idly
in the sun,
Break the silence, and the people whisper, awe-struck,
" It is done."

* The Declaration of Independence was really signed on
August 2d, 1775.

VII.

Then the dream began to vanish — burgesses, the war's
    red flames,
Charging Tarleton, proud Cornwallis, navies moving on
    the James,
Years of peace, and years of glory, all began to melt
    away,
And the statesman woke from slumber in the night, and
    tranquil lay, .
And his lips moved; friends there gathered with love's
    silken footstep near,
And he whispered, softly whispered in love's low and
    tender ear, —

VIII.

"It is the Fourth?"   "No, not yet," they answered,
    "but 'twill soon be early morn;
We will wake you, if you slumber, when the day begins
    to dawn."
Then the statesman left the present, lived again amid
    the past,
Saw, perhaps, the peopled future ope its portals grand
    and vast,
Till the flashes of the morning lit the far horizon low,
And the sun's rays o'er the forests in the east began to
    glow.

IX.

Rose the sun, and from the woodlands fell the midnight
    dews like rain,
In magnolias cool and shady sang the mocking-bird
    again,

And the statesman woke from slumber, saw the risen
    sun, and heard
Rippling breezes 'mid the oak-trees, and the lattice
    singing bird,
And, his eye serene uplifted, as rejoicing in the sun,
" It is the Fourth ? " his only question, — to the world
    his final one.

X.

Silence fell on Monticello — for the last dread hour was
    near,
And the old clock's measured ticking only broke upon
    the ear.
All the summer rooms were silent, where the great of
    earth had trod,
All the summer blooms seemed silent as the messengers
    of God ;
Silent were the hall and chamber where old councils oft
    had met,
Save the far boom of the cannon that recalled the
    old day yet.

XI.

Silent still is Monticello — he is breathing slowly now,
In the splendors of the noon-tide, with the death-dew
    on his brow ; —
Silent save the clock still ticking where his soul had
    given birth
To the mighty thoughts of freedom that should free
    the fettered earth ;
Silent save the boom of cannon on the sun-filled wave
    afar,
Bringing 'mid the peace eternal still the memory of war.

XII.

Evening in majestic shadows fell upon the fortress'
      walls ;

Sweetly were the last bells ringing on the James and
      on the Charles.

'Mid the choruses of freedom two departed victors lay,

One beside the blue Rivanna, one by Massachusetts
      Bay.

He was gone, and night her sable curtain drew across
      the sky ;

Gone his soul into all nations, gone to live and not to
      die.

FLAG OF TAUNTON GREEN.*

THE grand years have numbered one hundred and ten
    Since the first flag of freedom ascended the sky,
And the fair Green of Taunton made heroes of men,
    As men saw the ensign unfolding on high.
The motto of " Union and Liberty " rolled
Out into the sun-tide's vermilion and gold ;
And loud cried those heroes of liberty bold,
    " We'll defend with our valor and virtue and votes
            The red flag of Taunton,
            That waves o'er the Green."

'Twas autumn, bright autumn, and glimmered the weir,
    The Taunton flowed full on that beautiful day,
And kirtled wives gathered the flag-pole anear,
    'Mid the old men at prayer and the children at play.
They saw the red flag in blue Liberty's dome
Wave o'er the valley, Equality's home,
And they heard the men say, while their own lips were
        dumb,
    " We'll defend with our valor and virtue and votes
            The red flag of Taunton,
            That waves o'er the Green."

* The first flag of liberty was unfurled on the Green, at Taun
ton, Mass. — *Preble.*

The Taunton flowed swift through the shimmering weir,
   Past the rock where the Northmen came in from the
      Bay.
In the forest the red leaves were falling and sear,
   Where Annawan perished. The stone church to-day —
The loveliest church e'er the traveller saw,
   With its sentinel pines and its ivy-wreathed tower —
Stands hard by the place where the women in awe
   Heard their husbands cry out in that glorious hour,
   " We'll defend with our valor, our virtue and our votes,
      The red flag of Taunton,
      That waves o'er the Green."

The old parson stood by the church near the Green,
   And looked to the sky on that sun-flooded day;
The gray, rocky hill-side encircled the scene,
   And shaded streams rolled o'er the rocks to the Bay.
He lifted his hand, like a white cross, in prayer,
   And said, as the flag like an angel's wing spread,
" It is God who has written those words on the air;
   By the hand that has led you ye still shall be led.
   Long may valor and virtue defend with their votes
      The red flag that Taunton
      Has waved o'er the Green ! "

" Behold," said the parson, " its folds in the sky,
   In the eyes of the sun; do you know what you do?
The hand that sets Liberty's watchword on high
   Must to valor be pledged, and to honor be true.
Ye have set yonder flag for a sceptreless hand :
While God ye shall honor, your nation shall stand,
And when ye forsake Him shall perish the land.

Defend with your valor and virtue and votes
  The flag ye have lifted
  To-day o'er the Green."

" Peace ! "   How calmly the night of the past noon-tide
    shone
On the orchards of Taunton that glorious day,
As the mellow word rung like an altar-bell's tone.
  " Peace, peace, men of Taunton ! 'tis time we should
    pray.
O Thou whom all sceptres dost strengthen or break !
Yon flag to the hand of thy providence take :
In battle victorious, in peace glorious make,
  Defended by valor and virtue and votes,
      The flag we have lifted
      To-day o'er the Green."

The red flag of Taunton at old Brandywine
  Gave place to the flag of the stripes and the stars,
And the bold words of " Union and Liberty " shine
  No more as of old, 'mid the smoke-cloud of wars.
Here Liberty reigns, and her triumphs increase,
And our Union of States is the empire of peace,
And the sentinel's watch 'neath the flag does not cease,
  But virtue defends it with valor and votes,
      Like the heroes of Taunton
      That stood on the Green.

The grand years have numbered one hundred and ten
  Since the old flag of freedom ascended the sky,
And the fair Green of Taunton made heroes of men,
  As men saw the ensign unrolling on high.

An hundred and ten, and the new summer fills
Her gold horns of plenty, and banners the hills,
And the spirit of old still the patriot thrills,
    Still calling for valor and virtue and votes,
          While a million flags fly
          For that one on the Green.

PICTURES OF PLACES.

BISCAYNE BAY.

I.

I WALK alone on this mysterious night,
And feel that I am in the world alone ;
The palms around me lift their crowns of light :
In coral caves the faint-lipped waters moan,
And in my heart they find an answering tone,
On Biscayne Bay.

II.

Beyond the eye sweet sleep the Isles of June,
Crowns of the sea on night's imperial floors :
There dreams Bahama 'neath the rising moon,
A listless silence brooding o'er her shores,
The sea-breeze cools the fevered palms of noon
By Biscayne Bay.

III.

Afar I see like Christ's own jewelled hand
The Southern Cross in level distance, low,
A new discovered world seems sea and land,
A world Hesperian where strange splendors glow, —
As in the solitude I walk the sand
By Biscayne Bay.

IV.

Here years go on in endless summer days,
Alike in all breathes sweet the roses' breath,
Resplendent winter brings but fruitful rays.
Doth on these bright shores fall the shade of death,
Here, where the flowers fill all the winter ways —
On Biscayne Bay?

V.

Afar the ghostly sails move 'thwart the eye,
Afar 'mid mirrored stars tides opal flow,
The stars above, God's golden isles on high,
In deep reflections isled in deeps below,
They come, the phantom sails, and gleam and fly
From Biscayne Bay.

VI.

The air grows sweet, O wondrous sweet! and whence
Comes sweet the breath as if an angel passed?
It leads me on, the messenger of sense,
Past still lagoons of reeds like armies massed,
Wild orange groves, magnolia shades and thence
By Biscayne Bay,

VII.

To clouds of moss-hung cypresses, and there
I see the vines whose odors draw my feet,
And feel them breathe their sweetness on the air,
And meet them as glad souls life's angels meet,
These streaming jessamines 'mid boughs thin and bare
On Biscayne Bay.

VIII.

'Tis thus, O life, with influence, be it good,
Though 'mid the cypress shadows it may bloom
Or on dead rivers, fameless seas or flood,
'Twill reach some heart at last with its perfume,
Some lone heart find like mine amid the wood
    Of Biscayne Bay.

IX.

It may be mine to roam in solitude,
Or do my duty 'mid the hurrying crowd,
To stand the tide of life as I have stood,
Oft look for light to see a passing crowd,
But I may be a jessamine in the wood,
    Whate'er my way.

X.

'Tis acts that talk, and not the chattering tongue,
'Tis what we are that others bruise or bless,
And he may walk the ways by prophets sung
Who looks from evil unto righteousness,
His influence sweet as these dim odors flung
    On Biscayne Bay.

XI.

The silver ibis drifts across the sea,
And I towards my Northern home must turn.
I would be true, O blessed life, to thee;
With flowers I've seen the cold, dead cypress burn,
I would be true — long will thy memory be,
    O Biscayne Bay!

XII.

I leave thee, flower, to cheer the feet that stray
O'er the white corals of the long lagoon,
In flaming May-times of the winter day,
In glowing June-times of the winter morn,
The burning bush that met me on my way
          By Biscayne Bay.

          [Indian River, Florida.

ON THE SHORES OF THE BLUE MICHIGAN.

THE PIONEER OF CHICAGO.

My dead daughter's daughter, my own Gretchen Gray,
  The spring-time again has began,
I can hear the warm winds through the cotton-woods play
  On the shores of the blue Michigan.

The wind-flower is blooming ; I'm fourscore to-day,
  My dreams the eventful springs span
Since first as a boy on the star-grass I lay,
  On the shores of the blue Michigan.

The Illini's tents 'mid the green hazels burned,
  The deer through the cool sedges ran
As my boat from the pines of the Mackinaw turned
  Toward the shores of the blue Michigan.

I remember the day when the Great Council met, —
  The oak-leaves to fall had began ;
I saw the dark chiefs and their looks of regret
  As they stood by the blue Michigan.

And I saw near to-night, in the lone autumn light,
  Their plumes disappear till the van
Of the Illini old, in the showers of gold,
  Left behind them the blue Michigan.

Their plumes gray and white, at that coming of night,
 I saw the brown prairie span,
And fade on the dark as the even star's spark
 Lit the waves of the blue Michigan.

The Illini — theirs was what history unknown,
 What ages the eye could not scan !
I wept on that eve when the bugles were blown
 On the shores of the blue Michigan.

The crow from his crumbling nest watched them as slow
 The far trail they threaded ; and ran
The prairie-dogs 'mid the children, and low
 Sighed the reeds of the blue Michigan.

On, on to the West, to the Great River's tide,
 On, on 'neath the white stranger's ban,
And never the chief or the maid turned aside
 To look back on the blue Michigan.

All places are pleasant where good has been done,
 So the thought of young Nicholet ran,
As the Recollets' ways, 'neath the midsummer sun,
 He mapped on the blue Michigan.

'Twas a wilderness then : roamed the buffalo free
 In the ways seldom trodden by man,
And I planted my cabin and cotton-wood tree
 On the shores of the blue Michigan.

Then a village arose, then a town, and at last
   The spires of a city began
To hang their sweet bells o'er the wilderness vast
   And the waves of the blue Michigan.

I am fourscore to-day — like a vision it comes,
   I made for this city its plan,
And I built with these hands the first wilderness homes
   On the shores of the blue Michigan.

Men came, — whence I know not, — the world gathered
     here :
   Thence Progress her iron roads ran, —
And the steam-clouds, forever, in suns shining clear,
   Hung bright o'er the blue Michigan.

The city grew wondrous, her sails filled the lake,
   Her palaces trade here began ;
The hawk left the sky and the sedge-bird the brake.
   And Peace filled the blue Michigan.

Then I saw the brigades as they marched to the war ;
   The old flags the lake breezes fan ;
For Lincoln I heard the bells tolling in awe,
   On the shores of the blue Michigan.

I saw the red lake when the billows of fire
   O'er the marts and trade-palaces ran ;
When fell into ashes the temple and spire
   On the shores of the blue Michigan.

I am fourscore to-day, Gretchen Gray, Gretchen Gray,
　　And I made for this city its plan,
And I hear the west winds through the cotton-woods play,
　　As of old, on the blue Michigan.

But look! where she lies, the great heart of the West,
　　And offers his birthright to man,
And opens her gates to the peoples oppressed,
　　The pride of the blue Michigan;

Where labor is honor, and toil finds its due,
　　Where grows great humanity's plan; —
My dead daughter's daughter, my days will be few,
　　On the shores of the blue Michigan.

My days are but few, Gretchen Gray, Gretchen Gray;
　　And, when is accomplished life's span,
My form by the side of the pioneers lay,
　　On the shores of the blue Michigan.

I see her, fair city, the crown of the West,
　　That labor has builded for man.
My toils have been blest; and I ask but to rest
　　On the shores of the blue Michigan.

The wind-flower is blooming; I'm fourscore to-day,
　　My dreams the eventful years span
Since first as a boy on the star-grass I lay,
　　On the shores of the blue Michigan.

THE OLD FLOWER-BEDS.

[NEW ENGLAND.]

My grandmother's garden ! how well I remember
  That spot that delighted my eyes when a boy !
From the balm-breathing June to the mellowed Sep-
    tember,
  I hailed its fresh blossoms each morning with joy.

In fancy I see it when eve dark and chilly,
  O'ercasting the city, forbids me to roam :
In memory blossom the rose and the lily
  When solitude freshens the pictures of home.

I seem on the garden-gate swinging and singing,
  Or on the bars leaning in summer eves long ;
And, waiting my father his team homeward bringing,
  I list once again to the whippoorwill's song.

I remember the porch where the woodbine in clusters
  Of billowy green o'er the white roses hung ;
The swallows, whose purple and emerald lustres
  Shot swift through the air where the orioles sung.

O'er the old mossy wall, in the mellow airs blowing,
  The lilies made fragrant the evenings of May ;
And close by the door where the house-leeks were
    growing,
  My grandmother's garden, my pleasure-ground, lay.

Anear was the orchard, the moss to it clinging,
  The home of the birds and the banquet of bees :
I loved, in the spring-time, when church-bells were
      ringing,
  The peaceful white Sundays that came to the trees.

My grandmother's garden with green box was bordered ;
  There bloomed the blue myrtles, the first flowers of
      spring ;
There the peony's leaves seemed with pansies embroid-
      ered ;
  And hands of the fairies the bluebells to swing.

The balm-bed was there ; the sweets from its flowers
  The hummingbirds, gemming the air, came to draw :
And peeped from the woodbine and jessamine bowers
  The hives of the honey-bees golden with straw.

There oft, with her hymn-book, my grandmother wan-
      dered,
  Then seated herself in the arbor alone.
And read the old hymns and on holy themes pondered,
  While long on the hill-tops the western light shone.

The well-sweep was there in the elm-tree's broad
      shadow,
  And o'er it the golden-dressed orioles swung,
And a path from the old road and path from the meadow
  At the broad curb-stone met where the cool bucket
      hung.

They are gone, all are gone, whom that garden once
  gladdened :
No more shall I see them, — the young or the old :
Nor my grandmother's face with long memories sad-
  dened ;
  Her crown of bright silver is changed into gold.

Dimmer lights have the springs and the summers that
  follow ;
  The charm of the roses is not now as then ;
In duller gold skies flits the purple-winged swallow ;
  My heart ne'er will feel its old freshness again.

The joys youth expected were lost in the winning ;
  The distance enchanting from death's door is gone ;
And life a lost thread, like the fire-fly's, is spinning :
  I am lonely at night and am weary at morn.

But oft, with emotion that time doth not harden,
  I turn to my old home, its lessons recall ;
And the brightest of scenes is my grandmother's garden,
  Its pansies of spring, and its asters of fall.

And wherever I roam, in whatever bright harbor
  The anchor may drop, I remember with joy
The hymns that in summer-time rose from the arbor
  In that blooming garden when I was a boy.

CHOCORUA.

I.

I MOUNT Chocorua's granite stair;
　　Below the Conway meadows dream;
And, like pavilions of the air,
　　An hundred peaks around me gleam.
An hundred sun-crowned domes loom free,
　　Above the morn's mid-mountain mist,
Like rocky islands in a sea
　　Of pearl and gold and amethyst.

II.

Fair " Corway" of the mountain farms,
　　Red cottage homes 'mid fields of wheat;
The blue lakes slumber in thy arms,
　　The blue lakes ripple at thy feet.
An hundred vales below me glow,
　　Such vales as once the gods enticed;
I raise my charmèd eyes, and lo!
　　The air with hills seems paradised.

III.

Chocorua!　Chocorua!
　　Sharp peak that bids the step beware;
The wildest crag the foot can climb,
　　'Mid all these pinnacles of air.

Upon thy barren cone is heard
  No murmur of the world below;
The thin air cleaves no wing of bird,
  Nor harp of pine makes music low.

IV.

Lonely, proud-peaked Chocorua!
  Whose falling streams enchant my eye,
That lifts the venturous foot afar
  Towards the gardens of the sky;
Such heights as thine seemed formed to show
  The worth that in the spirit lies,
And lift the thought from things below
  To view the gates of Paradise!

V.

Wouldst thou be filled with high resolves?
  Go stand upon the mountain stair,
And pride shall vanish as dissolves
  The mist in morning's burning air.
A speck on Nature's rocky throne,
  Thou there shalt learn the spirit's worth,
And feel one answered prayer alone
  Is more than all the gains of earth.

THE CYPRESS GATES.

SLOWLY, boatman, slowly go;
Swift the leafy currents flow,
And I cannot see or know
What beyond yon dark wood waits,
Drifting toward the Cypress Gates
      Of the Ocklawaha.

We have passed funereal glooms,
Cypress caverns, haunted rooms,
Halls of gray moss starred with blooms —
Slowly, slowly in these straits,
Drifting toward the Cypress Gates
      Of the Ocklawaha.

In the towers of green o'erhead
Watch the vultures for the dead,
And below the egrets red
Eye the mossy pools like fates,
In the shadowy Cypress Gates
      Of the Ocklawaha.

Clouds of palm crowns lie behind,
Clouds of gray moss in the wind,
Crumbling oaks with jessamines twined,
Where the ring-doves meet their mates,
Cooing in the Cypress Gates
      Of the Ocklawaha.

High the silver ibis flies —
Silver wings in silver skies ;
In the sun the saurian lies ;
Comes the mocking-bird and prates
To the boatmen at the gates
     Of the Ocklawaha.

Nearer now, we're drawing near,
Naught but cypresses appear.
Hark, what song is that I hear !
'Tis a bird that love elates —
Some sweet bird beyond the gates
     Of the Ocklawaha.

Slowly — awful shades are these !
Seas of mosses, seas of trees !
Currents viewless as the breeze ;
Half the boat is in the straits,
Half is through the Cypress Gates
     Of the Ocklawaha.

On — the sunlight drops a ray !
On — the current knows the way !
On — the bird still sings its lay,
And a sun-flood fills the straits ; —
Shadows — shadows — were the gates
     Of the Ocklawaha.

Lo ! a shower of golden rain !
Lo ! the ibis flies again !
Runs the river toward the main,

Fades the dark air, fade the straits,
Fade the unlocked Cypress Gates
    Of the Ocklawaha.

Now the broader waters gleam —
Seems my voyage upon the stream
Like a semblance or a dream,
And the dream my soul elates;
Life flows through the Cypress Gates
    Like the Ocklawaha.

Will the ibis fly again?
Will the ring-dove sigh again?
Sunsets fall in golden rain?
Boatman, boatman, what awaits
Us beyond the Cypress Gates
    Of Life's Ocklawaha?

Boatman, boatman, oft I hear
Falling, falling on my ear,
One sweet voice that once was dear;
And I think God's love awaits
My poor faith beyond the gates
    Of the Ocklawaha.

Ibis, thou wilt fly again,
Ring-dove thou wilt sigh again,
Jessamines bloom in golden rain;
And a loving song-bird waits
Me beyond the Cypress Gates
    Of the Ocklawaha.

      [Originally published in the *Independent.*

CHICKAMAUGA.

AGAIN the summer fevered skies,
   The cooling autumn calms,
Again the golden moons arise
   On harvest-happy farms.
O nation free from sea to sea,
   With union blest forever,
Not vainly heroes fought for thee
   By Chickamauga River!

The autumn winds were piping low
   Beneath the vine-clad eaves ;
We heard the hollow bugle blow
   Among the ripened sheaves.
And fast the mustering squadrons passed
   Through mountain portals wide
And swift the blue brigades were massed
   By Chickamauga's tide.

It was the Sabbath ; and in awe
   We heard the dark hills shake,
And o'er the mountain turrets saw
   The smoke of battle break.
And 'neath that war-cloud, gray and grand,
   The hills o'erhanging low,
The Army of the Cumberland,
   Unequal, met the foe !

Again, O fair September night!
　Beneath the moon and stars,
I see, through memories dark and bright,
　The altar-fires of Mars.
The morning breaks with screaming guns
　From batteries dark and dire,
And where the Chickamauga runs
　Red runs the muskets' fire.

I see bold Longstreet's darkening host
　Sweep through our lines of flame,
And hear again, " The right is lost ! "
　Swart Rosecrans exclaim.
" But not the left," young Garfield cries ;
　" From that we must not sever,
While Thomas holds the field that lies
　On Chickamauga River ! "

Oh ! on that day of clouded gold,
　How, half of hope bereft,
The cannoneers, like Titans, rolled
　Their thunders on the left !
I see the battle-clouds again
　With glowing autumn's splendors blending ;
It seemed as if the gods with men
　Were on Olympian heights contending.

In dreams I stand beside the tide
　Where those old heroes fell.
Above the valleys, long and wide,
　Sweet rings the Sabbath bell.

I hear no more the bugle blow
　As on that fateful day;
I hear the ring-dove fluting low,
　Where shaded waters stray.

On Mission Ridge the sunlight streams
　Above the fields of fall,
And Chattanooga calmly dreams
　Beneath her mountain wall ;
Old Lookout Mountain towers on high,
　As in heroic days,
When 'neath the battle of the sky
　Were seen the summits blaze.

'Tis ours to lay no garlands fair
　On many graves unknown,
Kind Nature sets her gentians there,
　And fall the sear leaves lone.
Those heroes' graves no shaft of Mars
　May mark with beauty ever ;
But floats the flag of forty stars
　By Chickamauga River.

AMERICAN HOLIDAYS, FESTIVALS, AND THE SCHOOL-ROOM.

THE NATION'S DEFENDERS.

ODE FOR JULY 4.

AGAIN wake the song to the nation's defenders,
    The years of prosperity rise and increase ;
The summer days glow with their shadowless splendors,
    And blow the war-bugles the sweet notes of peace.
Here, here where the Northmen their harbored sail
        shifted,
    And wondering turned to the dark seas again,
And the knights of the Fleur-de-lis gallantly lifted
    The banners of Francis — awake the glad strain
        To the valor of old,
        To the flag we behold,
And the twice twenty stars that our banners unfold !

Sing the Pilgrims of old, who, by dark foes surrounded,
    Their lone, tentless way through the still forests trod,
Who knelt by the Charles and our Ilion founded
    On the hills where their faces were lifted to God !
Sing, sing them, these heroes of history glorious,
    Who caught the free spirit of Cromwell and Vane,
And over the foes of their empire victorious
    Throned Liberty monarch — awake the glad strain

To the valor of old,
To the flag we behold,
And the twice twenty stars that our banners unfold!

Defenders of Might to King George's towns loyal,
   When o'er them the Red Cross of Albion blew ;
Defenders of Right, in humanity royal,
   Beneath the white stars of the century new.
They stood as one man when the Red Cross was o'er
      them,
   They stood as one man 'neath the new flag again ;
The years glowed behind them, the years glowed
      before them,
   And shall glow forever — awake the glad strain
            To the valor of old,
            To the flag we behold,
And the twice twenty stars that our banners unfold!

Sing, sing them who fell by each palm-shaded river,
   The Union to save and the bondmen to free!
The mocking-bird sings by their graves, and forever
   When valor awakes they remembered shall be.
Their deeds thrill our lives, their examples the ages,
   And shadowless ever their fame shall remain ;
The white marbles bloom for their sakes, and the pages
   Of history gladden with hope — wake the strain
            To the valor of old,
            To the flag we behold,
And the twice twenty stars that our banners unfold!

Then sing ye the song of the nation's defenders,
   The wild roses bloom and the Western winds blow,
The natal day hail that to memory renders
   The debt that to Liberty's martyrs we owe !
In spirit they come when the bugles are blowing
   The sweet notes of peace on our festival days;
In spirit they live in the great empires growing,
   And shall live forever ! — sing, sing ye the praise
             Of the valor of old,
             Of the flag we behold,
And the twice twenty stars that our banners unfold !

[Originally published in *Congregationalist.*

.

LET THE CHORUS OF HILLS.

THANKSGIVING.

I.

O THOU whose love breathed on the spring-time its
       breath,
  And shed on the autumn its beams,
Thy word is our hope, and the cup of our faith
  We dip in Thy measureless streams.
    Let the chorus of hills wake the wonderful strain,
      Let the autumn respond to the spring;
    Break forth into anthems of gladness again,
      And boundless beneficence sing.

II.

Alike is Thy goodness in sunshine and rain,
  Alike when we see Thee or trust,
Alike when the harvests illumine the plain,
  And the seeds are the graves of the dust.

    Let the chorus of hills, etc.

III.

Thy grace is a sun, and its seasons are love,
  Thy mercies forever endure,
And seed-time and harvest eternally prove
  Thy promise unfailing and sure,

    Let the chorus of hills, etc.

LABOR DAY.

THE PLOUGHSHARES OF THE WEST.

I.

HEART of the West, I love thee,
　Thy pulses grand and free,
Thy sails of progress as they move
　Across the floral sea.
The pen of art, that song indites,
　May stir the gentler breast,
But history's noblest pages writes
　The ploughshare of the West.

II.

Go, poet, to each ancient land,
　That old romances sway,
Where pages in throne shadows stand,
　And sweet their suave lutes play,
Then westward turn from oilless lights,
　Time's latest sun is best;
The nation's noblest poem writes
　The ploughshare of the West.

III.

The world's best hands now drive the plough,
　The soil king's, freedom-crowned,
And man's imperial chariots now
　Are those that break the ground.

The rime, the rune, the saga old
    May be the hermit's quest,
But man's best promise writes the bold
    Brave ploughshare of the West.

IV.

Here nature plays the pipes of Pan,
    And health and honor sing;
A Cincinnatus is each man,
    And every man a king.
With conscience free his God to find,
    His shrine his open breast,
The farmer follows for mankind
    The ploughshare of the West.

V.

Plough on, plough on, till justice rule;
    Plough, for the ages wait;
Plough for the church, plough for the school,
    Plough for the hall of State;
Plough, like the hand of Lincoln, plough,
    Like Garfield, for the best,
And map the fields of nations now,
    Ye ploughshares of the West.

VI.

'Neath skies of Hope's eternal blue,
    Plough for the flag that waves
For Irish tenant, Russian Jew,
    For Cuba's isle of slaves;

Plough for the peoples yet to be,
   For every life oppressed;
The furrows stretch from sea to sea,
   Ye ploughshares of the West.

VII.

Then hail forever, sons of toil,
   And hail the work ye do,
Thy field the great republic's soil,
   And brown thy royal hue.
And hail ye cabin-palace gates
   That ope to every guest;
All hail! Heaven's noblest blessing waits
   The ploughshares of the West.

.

MEMORIAL DAYS.

SET THE FLAG ON THEIR GRAVES.

PLAY the peace-bugles low,
  While the white lilies blow,
And the apple-blooms fill
  The green valleys with snow;
Let our sweet songs arise
  On the spring's western wind;
We can never forget them
  Who died for mankind.

        Set the flag on their graves,
          In the lilies enshrined;
        We can never forget them
          Who died for mankind.

Set the flag on their graves,
  Where the vernal wind laves
The roses of peace
  From the far western waves;
'Tis for you and for me
  Their sweet lives they resigned;
They are brothers of all men
  Who died for mankind.

Set the flag on their graves,
  In the lilies enshrined;
They are brothers of all men
  Who died for mankind.

Set the flag on their graves,
  And the thrush, floating low,
Shall take up our song
  And sing on as we go,
O'er the emblem we leave
  'Mid the lilies enshrined;
Their lives are immortal
  Who died for mankind.

Set the flag on their graves,
  In the lilies enshrined;
Their lives are immortal
  Who died for mankind.

ARBOR-DAY SONG.

I.

LET other lands of knighthood sing!
  Thou art my song, America;
In thee each free-born soul is king,
  In freedom and America!
      Strong were the hands that planted thee,
      Grand was the Mayflower on the sea,
      That bore the seed of Liberty
  To thee, the world's America!

In Freedom's air we plant the tree,
  Our land of hope, America.
    Beneath the blue sky, Freedom's dome,
    Within the green earth, Freedom's home,
    We plant the tree for years to come,
  And pray, God bless America!

II.

The ages waited long for thee,
  Our own, our own America,
Then rose the pilot of the sea,
  America, America!

He saw the stars prophetic shine,
And dreamed the earth a star divine,
And found, beyond the horizon's line,
Thy happy isles, America !

> *In Freedom's air we plant the tree, etc.*

III.

Hope set the school-house by the home,
　Our own, our own America ;
Faith left in air her golden dome,
　America, America !
　　And where our fathers knelt to pray,
　　The crownèd cities rise to-day,
　　And Progress makes her outward way,
　Heart of the West, America !

> *In Freedom's air we plant the tree, etc.*

IV.

Let other lands of knighthood sing !
　Thou art my song, America ;
In each free-born soul is crowned a king,
　In my own land, America !
　　I love thy homes where honor dwells,
　　The honest toil that commerce swells ;
　　I love thy old New England bells,
　My own, my own America !

MISSISSIPPI DAY.

I.

O TIME! O change! how have these prairies altered
  Since those dim, distant days
When, tranced with beauty, lonely Allouez faltered
  In his uncertain ways;

II.

Since on these streams the dark-robed Jesuits drifted
  Far from the crystal seas,
And knighted sea-kings on the blue lakes lifted
  The silver fleur-de-lis!

III.

Here prayed Marquette, by ancient tribes surrounded
  In forest ways untrod,
And lonely Jolliet mighty cities founded,
  Where first he talked with God,

IV.

Far from the Huron's many-foliaged village,
  Far from the Iroquois,
Far from the scenes of rapine, hate, and pillage,
  Beside the Illinois.

V.

They saw the land with peace and plenty growing,
  On rolled the river fair,
And seas of flowers o'er endless shallows flowing,
  And seas of odorous air.

VI.

The lonely chief upon his pine-plumed eyrie
  Gazed o'er the sea of blooms,
And watched the strange sail as it wandered weary
  Amid the twilight glooms.

VII.

The bison, cooling in the stream before them,
  Fled to the dark oak's shade ;
The wondering eagle wheeled on slant wing o'er them ;
  Their sails the warm winds swayed.

VIII.

Still on and on the dark priests wandered, praying
  And singing hymns of praise,
And on and on the river rolled, displaying
  Its grand march to their gaze.

IX.

Then came La Salle his water-chariot driving
  Triumphal down the tide,
And, hard against the imprisoned currents striving,
  Rode on the ocean wide.

X.

O cross that marched into the sunset gleaming,
   Down from the northern seas,
That nations followed wondering and dreaming—
   The silvery fleur-de-lis,

XI.

The red cross flags, the cour-de-bois, the ranger,
   The knight, the chevalier,
The poor of earth, the exile freed from danger,
   The lonely pioneer, —

XII.

Faith still beholds thee on the waters glowing
   In twilight's amber air,
While Marquette walks the uncertain waves, yet know-
      ing
   That God is with him there!

CHILDREN'S DAY.*

O CHILDREN'S Day in the summer's prime,
   How bright is the world and how fair,
When over the bowers the roses climb,
   And the lilies are waving in air!
We bring to our altars our gifts of flowers
   And the singing birds, and say
The happiest day of the summer hours
   Is the Children's Sabbath Day!
The Sabbath of lilies and roses!
   Our souls draw near in praises
To the beauty of Christ in Paradise,
   On the Children's Sabbath Day!

To-day the censers of roses swing,
   More sweet than the censers of gold;
The birds at the altar sweetly sing
   As they sung in the temple of old.
We joyfully sing 'mid the birds and flowers
   To the praise of God, and say
The beautiful time of the summer hours
   Is the Children's Sabbath Day!

* Originally written for music by Professor Sherwin, published by John Church & Co.

The Sabbath of lilies and roses!
　Our souls draw near in praises
To the beauty of Christ in Paradise,
　On the Children's Sabbath Day!

O who is the Rose of Sharon to-day?
　And who is the Lily white?
And whose is the love that leads our way
　To the gardens of Paradise bright?
At His feet triumphant we cast our flowers,
　And our off'rings there we lay,
Rejoicing the gifts of His love are ours
　On the Children's Sabbath Day!
The Sabbath of lilies and roses!
　Our souls draw near in praises
To the beauty of Christ in Paradise,
　On the Children's Sabbath Day!

THE OLD SCHOOL-ROOM.

THE BEAUTIFUL VILLAGE OF YULE.

My spring-time of life has departed ;
　　Its romance has ended at last :
My dreamings were once of the future,
　　But now they are all of the past.
And memory oft in my trials
　　Goes back to my pastimes at school,
And pictures the children who loved me,
　　In the beautiful village of Yule.

The school-house still stands by the meadow,
　　And green is the spot where I played,
And flecked with the sun is the shadow
　　Of the evergreen woods where I strayed.
The thrush in the meadowy places
　　Still sings in the evergreens cool ;
But changed are the fun-loving faces
　　Of the children who met me at Yule.

I remember the day when, a teacher,
　　I met those dear faces anew ;
The warm-hearted greetings that told me
　　The friendships of childhood are true.

I remember the winters I struggled,
  When care-worn and sick, in my school :
I remember the children who loved me,
  In the beautiful village of Yule.

So true, in the days of my sadness,
  Did the hearts of my trusted ones prove,
My sorrow grew light in the gladness
  Of having so many to love.
I gave my own heart to my scholars,
  And banished severity's rule ;
And happiness dwelt in my school-room,
  In the beautiful village of Yule.

I taught them the goodness of loving
  The beauty of nature and art ;
They taught me the goodness of loving
  The beauty that lies in the heart.
And I prize more than lessons of knowledge
  The lessons I learned in my school, —
The warm hearts that met me at morning,
  And left me at evening, in Yule.

I remember the hour that we parted ;
  I told them, while moistened my eye,
That the bell of the school-room of glory
  Would ring for us each in the sky.
Their faces were turned to the sunset,
  As they stood 'neath the evergreens cool ;
I shall see them no more as I saw them
  In the beautiful village of Yule.

The bells of the school-room of glory
  Their summons have rung in the sky.
The moss and the fern of the valley
  On some of the old pupils lie:
Some have gone from the wearisome studies
  Of earth to the happier school;
Some faces are bright with the angels',
  Who stood in the sunset at Yule.

I love the instructions of knowledge,
  The teachings of nature and art,
But more than all others the lessons
  That come from an innocent heart.
And still to be patient and loving
  And trustful I hold as a rule,
For so I was taught by the children
  Of the beautiful village of Yule.

My spring-time of life has departed;
  Its romance has ended at last:
My dreamings were once of the future,
  But now they are all of the past.
Methinks, when I stand in life's sunset,
  As I stood when we parted at school,
I shall see the bright faces of scholars
  I loved in the village of Yule.

BRADFORD OF AUSTERFIELD.

I.

A WANDERER from the Western land,
  From cities o'er the seas,
I stood one day in Scrooby's Manor,
  Beneath the ancient trees.

II.

My thoughts were from the ruins turned;
  I saw that elder day,
When in the hall of Scrooby's Manor
  The Pilgrims met to pray.

III.

I saw a lonely orphan boy,
  With face serene and fair,
Walk day by day to Scrooby's Manor
  And join the Pilgrims there.

IV.

Sweet rang the bells of Austerfield;
  He heeded not the call,
But day by day in Scrooby's Manor
  He sought the chapel hall.

v.

Grave men were they, with faces firm,
  His face was young and fair —
They formed a church at Scrooby's Manor —
  A nation born was there.

vi.

He sleeps upon the Pilgrim hill.
  Precisioner was he?
A ruin old is Scrooby's Manor;
  He built beyond the sea.

THE GRAVE OF PENN.

WHAT though above the Schuylkill gleams
    For him no shaft of fame,
What though amid these English streams
    We find his unsought name!

We know his country was the earth,
    His countrymen mankind ;
And where his death or where his birth,
    We need not seek or find.

Above the world his quiet mind
    Poised on its wings of trust ;
He lived for all, and left behind
    The memory of the just.

Allotted by an unseen hand,
    Time gives his work its dowers ;
His soul, a Western empire grand,
    His body, English flowers.

Self-sacrifice is never lost,
    But bears its own reward ;
They who for others leave the most,
    Shall have the most from God.

His influence well has filled the earth.
    He needs no marble tomb ;
But fitly for his modest worth
    The English daisies bloom.

ZINZENDORF, ON DEPARTING FOR AMERICA.

I.

Ye say the Golden Age is gone,
    The lyres immortal sleep;
No Argo at the crimson morn
    Hails life's Ægean deep;

II.

The seers no longer dwell with men,
    Old oracles are dumb;
But light shall fill the world again —
    The Golden Age 's come.

III.

The church her greatest triumphs waits,
    And I can almost hear
The nations at the open gates
    Of heaven, as they draw near.

IV.

Those who've believed since Christ arose,
    Received the Bethlehem story,
Are as an ocean's drop to those
    Who yet shall see his glory.

v.

And so I willing leave the Rhine,
   A wilderness to brave,
And welcome, in the Light Divine,
   The Susquehanna's wave.

vi.

I feel the breeze celestial blow,
   The tides celestial run,
And to my post of faith I'll go
   Beneath the setting sun.

vii.

For Christ an exile far I'll roam,
   For Him I'll cross the sea;
My Lord's commands are more than home
   And more than life to me.

viii.

Not half the gospel, but the whole,
   Upon my heart I bear;
Not half the world, but every soul,
   I seek on wings of prayer.

ix.

All souls to me have equal worth,
   In all I brothers find;
The Cross that shines above the earth
   Arose for all mankind.

X.

Farewell to thee, my native coast,
 And welcome shores untrod ;
They who for others seek the most,
 Shall find the ways of God.

THE SCHOOL-HOUSE STANDS BY THE FLAG.

I.

Ye who love the Republic, remember the claim
Ye owe to her fortunes, ye owe to her name.
To her years of prosperity past and in store,
A hundred behind you, a thousand before.
  'Tis the school-house that stands by the flag,
    Let the nation stand by the school ;
  'Tis the school-bell that rings for our Liberty old,
    'Tis the school-boy whose ballot shall rule.

II.

The blue arch above us is Liberty's dome,
The green fields beneath us, Equality's home.
But the school-room to-day is Humanity's friend, —
Let the people the flag and the school-house defend.
  'Tis the school-house that stands by the flag,
    Let the nation stand by the school ;
  'Tis the school-bell that rings for our Liberty old,
    'Tis the school-boy whose ballot shall rule.

SONG OF THE NEW ENGLAND HAY-FIELD.

In the days of my youth, I remember,
  An old mower sang me this rune:
"The aftermath of the September
  Is not the sweet clover of June."
And he said, "Whatever thy station,
  Whatever thy hands may employ,
Be true to thy best inspiration:
  'Tis thy angel of blessings, my boy."
Then swift rung his scythe, that old farmer's,
  And fast fell the grass to the rune,
"The aftermath of the September
  Is not the sweet clover of June."

The osprey's green wings drifted o'er me,
  On the sun-tides, while, glinting below,
The bobolinks toppled before me,
  And the wind blew the daisies like snow.
All nature seemed filled with elation,
  And the old farmer whistled for joy:
"'Tis the fruit of life's young inspiration
  That fills life with gladness, my boy."

And, his scythe all embedded with flowers,
   He piled up the grass to the rune,
"The aftermath of the September
   Is not the sweet clover of June."

The gray walls with roses were glowing,
   The blue lilies breathing below :
Afar were the meadow brooks flowing
   By the mill, in the high noon aglow.
And he said, while the herons wheeled over,
   And screamed in the sun in their joy,
"The air is all fragrant with clover :
   'Twas clover I planted, my boy."
And on paced the red-shirted farmer,
   And on fell the grass to the rune,
"The aftermath of the September
   Is not the sweet clover of June."

"'Tis the spring-time that glows with endeavor,
   And gives to young purpose its power ;
The sun of the autumn will never
   Bring forth the ripe fruit from the flower.
Though the aftermath springs from the clover,
   The clover comes not from the fern :
Give thy hand to thy best inspiration, —
   Thy spring-time will never return."
And on swept the scythe of the farmer,
   And on fell the grass to the rune,
"The aftermath of the September
   Is not the sweet clover of June."

One day, when September was burning,
    I met the old farmer again,
The thin swaths of the aftermath turning
    Where once the thick clover had lain.
And gone were roses and lilies,
    One lone robin sang in the tree :
" It is clover that comes from the clover,
    But the first yield was double, you see."
And he rifled his scythe, that old farmer,
    And cut the thin grass to the rune,
" The aftermath of the September
    Is not the sweet clover of June."

" Ah ! youth is no season for leisure, —
    Too wide its horizons expand :
In thy purpose and struggle find pleasure
    That is worthy the brain and the hand.
And hold as the wiles of the tempter
    Whatever that purpose debars :
The lamps of the red billiard palace
    Are not the white lights of the stars."
And rung his old scythe to the rifle,
    And cut the thin grass to the rune,
" The aftermath of the September
    Is not the sweet clover of June."

The years of my youth are all ended,
    The old man sleeps under the fern ;
But oft the long days of my childhood
    And the rune of the hay-field return.

'Tis the seed of the spring that has promise, —
   The choicest seed, bounteously sown ;
And the breath of the spring-time will never
   Come back to the fields that are mown.
And over and over and over
   My years bring the thought of the rune,
That no aftermath sweet of the clover
   Is like the sweet clover of June.

CRYSTAL, SILVER, AND GOLD.

(WEDDING ANNIVERSARIES.)

I.

LOVE is the secret of success,
And love alone is happiness;
  Where'er life's lot may be
Some true hearts hear the marriage chimes,
And some at gracious dates and times
Their wedding's anniversary chimes—
     'The crystal chimes,
     The silver chimes,
The mellowed tones of golden chimes.
  And sweet for thee of whom I sing
  May all the bells of concord ring—
     The crystal chimes,
     The silver chimes,
The mellowed tones of golden chimes.

II.

Five times three years depart, and then
  The early chimes of crystal ring;
The wedding chimes recall again
  And end the budded marriage spring.
In household trees the robin sings,
The swallow comes on purple wings,

The May time deepens into June;
In lustrous skies hangs low the moon,
The lilacs toss in scented air,
Red grows the peach-tree, white the pear,
    And o'er the mossy orchard wall
    The orchard's flaky blossoms fall;
Love's song may change to lullabies,
Her kisses fall on little eyes,
    And cares and prayers be multiplied.
        If so it be, if so it be,
        Ring sweet, ring sweet,
                O crystal chimes !
        And ring the blithe-lipped
                Silver chimes.

III.

When five and twenty years are spent,
    Love's silver chimes shall fill the air,
    And time shall answer half thy prayer,
And life shall pitch her half-way tent;
    The fire-flies then at dewy eve
    Their threads of gold no more shall weave;
The roses fall, the crowned sheaves shine,
The emerald clusters fill with wine ;
    The silver on thy fair child's brow
    Against thy silver locks may bow,
And it may be, as years have rolled,
The bell some household life has tolled :
    Some heart to whom thy breast did yearn
    God's hand have covered with the fern.

Some early go away, some late,
Some long to guard the fireside wait,
    And some must follow — it is well.
    Strike tenderly, O funeral bell !
May warm love greet you when the chimes
Shall ring their five and twenty times.

IV.

The golden chimes of fifty years !
    Few hear the golden chimes, and yet
    Some wear Time's silver coronet,
Before the brighter crown appears.
    Serenely then life's autumn light
    Falls on the azure verge of night.
Before the north wind, in the skies,
Spring's purple swallow voiceless flies
    The crowns of later harvests burn,
    The violets blue to gentians turn ;
The tides of love still onward flow,
Before the fire young faces glow ;
    And multiplied the joy of years
    In children's children's smiles appears,
The lips of age still warm lips press
And drink the wine of happiness ;
    In Simeon's song of praise of old
    The joy that fills the heart is told ;
The cradle by the arm-chair stands
And little hands clasp wrinkled hands.
    Ah ! blest are they to whom appears
    This long serenity of years,

Recalling all life's dates and times.
 So may it be, so may it be,
And Love's sweet chimes at all her times
 Be rung for thee, be rung for thee.

v.

And are these other chimes to ring
 In life's cymballium, when sweet
The nola bells of childhood's morns,
And youth's melodious carillons.
And marriage bells, that ring between
The signum bells and bells compline,
 The melodies of time complete?
 Fair hands may set the marriage clock,
What time we never can forget ;
 No key the future can unlock,
No hand the clock of death may set.
O chimes more sweet than crystal chimes,
O chimes more sweet than silver chimes,
Or mellowness of golden chimes !
I hear the Hebrew prophet sing
Of Beulah's land, where married are
 All constant hearts, and John proclaim
Upon the lone Ægean sea
 The marriage supper in Christ's name,
And speak of melodies afar,
 Celestial bells of mystery.
You journey toward far Salem's wall,
 From youth's fair land of Galilee.
One day, one day, life's tent will fall
 Before God's temple gate. O ye

Who vows begin and vows renew,
And happy years of life review,
  May Love's sweet chimes,
  At all her times,
 Where'er life's tent of peace may be, ·
  Be rung for thee,
  Be rung for thee,
Till life shall end, and after life
 The bells of immortality —
  The crystal chimes,
  The silver chimes,
The melodies of golden chimes,
And those sweet bells,
  For thee, for thee,
 John heard on the Ægean sea.

DECORATION DAY.

I.

WHENE'ER we meet the friends once fondly cherished,
  And hand all warm with old affection take,
Then let us breathe the names of those who perished
  On fields of honor, for their country's sake.

II.

They come no more when spring-time birds are singing,
  When trills the swallow 'neath the shady eaves,
When light in air the summer bells are swinging
  Above the ripple of the tender leaves.

III.

They come no more when bugles sweet are blowing
  The notes of peace, on Freedom's natal days;
They hear no more, in softened numbers flowing,
  The strain that tells the patriot hero's praise.

IV.

They come no more when village bells are ringing
  In fragrant airs, above the river calm;
They join no more the tuneful voices singing,
  At rosy eve, the old familiar psalm.

V.

They come no more when festive boards are laden,
  They smile no more when Friendship charms the
    hours,
They meet no more with airy step the maiden
  Whom loving hands have diademed with flowers.

VI.

'Tis ours to smile on other lips of beauty,
  To other hearts in happy days to turn ;
'Twas theirs to perish on the field of duty,
  And rest in silence 'neath the moss and fern.

VII.

They gave their all : — our love to them returning
  Shall make an altar near their ashes still,
When Sabbath sunsets on the vale are burning,
  And summer twilights fade upon the hill.

VIII.

One manly form still haunts my recollection,
  Whose life with mine through even boyhood lay,
Who well may claim the tribute of affection
  Beside these hills, where shaded waters stray.

IX.

We all recall his youthful aspirations
  To do some worthy deed to bless mankind ;
He gave his own fair life to save the nation's,
  And left a stainless memory behind.

X.

The school-bell's music floats across the river,
  The church-bell's music o'er the valley steals,
But we shall see his pleasant features never,
  Till sweet above the bell of glory peals.

XI.

O give such mounds the blessing of protection,
  There make a shrine a lofty aim to learn,
When summer gives the flowers a resurrection,
  And hangs her jewels on the moss and fern.

XII.

Let Love there mingle her sweet tears with Pity,
  Let Aspiration there be newly born,
And Fancy follow to the Golden City,
  In pensive hours, the feet heroic gone.

OH, BLEST ARE THEY.

OH, blest are they whose lives are nobly ended,
  No dark dishonor shall they e'er receive;
From peril flown, to God's pure light ascended,
  Victorious through the ages long to live.
            Cease from thy sorrows, cease!
            They rest in perfect peace;
  Sweetly they rest, and their works do follow them.

Their lives more lovely made our world of beauty,
  Their death has made the spirit world more bright.
And long their mem'ry, in our hours of duty,
  Shall, like near angels, turn our steps aright.
            Cease from thy sorrows, cease!
            They rest in perfect peace;
  Sweetly they rest, and their works do follow them.

Gone to the city of unshaded splendor,
  Gone to the world where earthly labors cease,
They gave to us the best that life could render,
  And wait our coming at Christ's doors of peace.
            Then from thy sorrows cease!
            They rest in perfect peace;
  Sweetly they rest, and their works do follow them.

[Written for music; by permission of John Church & Co.
Sung at the funeral of Garfield at Cincinnati.]

THE EMIGRANT BABY'S SMILE.

I.

THE great ocean steamer comes into the bay,
  And the flag-blooming haven it nears ;
On the bright sunny deck is a baby at play
With the shade of the flag as it passes its way,
  And it laughs at the emigrant's cheers.
  " Smile on, little one, on thy sun-lighted way ;
  O'er the seas and the flowers to the Georgian Bay,
    My emigrant baby, smile.

II.

"The future is waiting with blessings for thee,
  To give and to not take away,
The west wind is blowing the flag of the free ;
The flag of Prosperity stands by the Sea,
  And church spire of Peace by the Bay.
  Then smile on, little one, on thy sun-lighted way ;
  O'er the seas and the flowers to the Georgian Bay,
    O emigrant baby, smile.

III.

"Where labor is honor and title is worth,
  And naught can dishonor but guile,

Where each is a noble by right of his birth,
And free as the sky lies the empire of earth,
  My emigrant baby, smile.
Oh, well may'st thou smile on thy sun-lighted way ;
O'er the seas and the flowers to the Georgian Bay,
  My own little emigrant, smile !"

BESIDE THE ORGAN.

I.

THE organ rose mute in its garments of sable,
    And silent beside it the master lay dead ;
There were harps of white lilies on altar and table,
    And crosses, art-broken, that faint perfume shed.
The May-flowers' breath on the sobbing air trembled,
    And fast fell the tears that affection had won,
Then the preacher spake low to the weepers assembled —
    " He is only remembered for what he has done."

II.

The casket, that over the Rhine and the ocean
    Had borne the frail form, with white roses was
        spread ; *
And 'neath the great organ that erst to emotion
    The master had wakened, it prisoned the dead.
Here, here where he toiled, was his last journey ended,
    The journey unconscious of shadow or sun ;
And sweetly the words of the preacher ascended —
    " He is only remembered for what he has done."

III.

He gave to the world — 'twas the best he could render —
    A spirit of beauty, a spirit of love ;

* G. Astor Broad.   The quotation is from Dr. Bonar.

To each trust he was true, to each need he was tender,
  And his wing swiftly passed to the brightness above.
He lived for his Art, as the child for the mother;
  He used it for God, like a dutiful son.
He died, and a thousand hearts wept for a brother,
  Yet only remembered for what he had done.

THE DEAD PUPIL.

I.

OR if at eve life's frail tent fall,
  Or 'neath the noonday sun,
It is a blessing to recall
  A life-work nobly done.
And they in endless influence live
Who blessed lives to others give.

II.

Though short the mission that may fill
  The life of purity,
The memory is an angel still,
  And will forever be.
And though no more we hear the voice,
That once it spake our hearts rejoice.

III.

The memory of the good though brief
  Is an eternal star;
And it shall rise on nights of grief
  Forever from afar, —
Whate'er for it may be God's will,
A good life is a blessing still.

IV.

For thee, fair Soul, for whom we weep,
   — A broken flower in bloom —
Who in life's bridal robes doth sleep,
   In silence, in the tomb,
Thou wert our joy, and thou shalt be
Our angel still in memory.

V.

The shadows fall for us ; for thee
   The gates immortal ope ;
Thou art with the Beloved, and He,
   Our Comforter and Hope,
Abides with us — we own His will —
Thy presence is an angel still.

VI.

Death's shadows fall from light divine,
   Regret upsprings from worth,
And tearful thoughts of lives like thine
   Are heavenly seeds on earth.
The eyelids droop in long regret,
But memory brings an angel yet.

APPENDIX.

THANKSGIVING FOR AMERICA.

THE nobility and cavaliers in attendance on the court, together with the authorities of the city, came to the gates to receive him, and escorted him to the royal presence. Ferdinand and Isabella were seated with their son, Prince John, under a superb canopy of state, awaiting his arrival. On his approach, they rose from their seats, and, extending their hands to him to salute, caused him to be seated before them. These were unprecedented marks of condescension to a person of Columbus' rank, in the haughty ceremonies of the court of Castile. It was indeed the proudest moment in the life of Columbus. — *Prescott.*

Columbus pointed out (to Ferdinand and Isabella) the opportunities afforded to Christian zeal, for the illumination of a race of men whose minds, far from being wedded to any system of idolatry, were prepared by their extreme simplicity for the reception of pure and uncorrupted doctrine. The last consideration touched Isabella's heart most sensibly ; and the whole audience, kindled with various emotions by the speaking eloquence, filled up the perspective with the gorgeous coloring of their own fancy, as ambition, or avarice, or devotional feeling, predominated in their bosoms. When Columbus ceased, the king and queen, together with all present, prostrated themselves on their knees in grateful thanksgivings, while the solemn strains of the *Te Deum* were poured forth by the choir of the royal chapel, as in commemoration of some glorious victory. — *Prescott.*

COLUMBUS' DAY.

In Madrid the 12th of October was a great day — there they celebrated with a *fête* the anniversary of the day that gave to Castile and Leon a new world, which, however, Castile and Leon could not manage to retain. But who ever heard of an American celebration of the 12th of October? But it is a twelfth-night ! — it was in the night that a ray of light from San Salvador struck a bliss upon Colon's eyes as he paced the deck of the *Pinta* — which should be celebrated, next to our two great Christian festivals, above all others. Yet, though it is one of the few historical days that are sure beyond controversy, and though it commemorates the kingly virtues of undaunted courage, persistence, faith, culminating in the discovery of a world, the day passes and is scarcely mentioned ; the great dailies of New York, in their greatness, give us several columns of crime and scandal, but not a word for Colon's day. It deserves better treatment, and we hope will get it, and to that end we renew our suggestion that it be made a national Thanksgiving Day. — *Christian at Work.*

GUILLAUME.

Dr. Mackay tells the story thus : —

WILLIAM THE CONQUEROR.

I.

GREAT King William spread before him
    All his stores of wealth untold,
Diamonds, emeralds, and rubies,
    Heaps on heaps of minted gold.
Mournfully he gazed upon it
    As it glitter'd in the sun,
Sighing to himself, " Oh, treasure !
    Held in care, by sorrow won.
Millions think me rich and happy,
    But, alas ! before me piled,
I would give thee ten times over
    For the slumbers of a child."

II.

Great King William from his turret
    Heard the martial trumpets blow,
Saw the crimson banners floating
    Of a countless host below ;
Saw their weapons flash in sunlight,
    As the squadrons trod the sward ;
And he sigh'd, " Oh, mighty army !
    Hear thy miserable lord :
At my word thy legions gather, —
    At my nod thy captains bend, —
But, with all thy power and splendor,
    I would give thee for a friend ! ''

III.

Great King William stood on Windsor,
  Looking from its castled height
O'er his wide-spread realm of England,
  Glittering in the morning light;
Looking on the tranquil river
  And the forest waving free,
And he sigh'd, "Oh, land of beauty!
  Fondled by the circling sea,
Mine thou art, but I would yield thee,
  And be happy, could I gain,
In exchange, a peasant's garden
  And a conscience free from stain.'

CHAMPLAIN.

THE leading thoughts of this poem were expressed in Champlain's last letters to Richelieu and to his friends in France.

"The conversion of a single soul is of more value than an empire." — *Champlain.*

SIR HENRY VANE AT SCILLY.

HIS imprisonment at Scilly continued about two years. While waiting the slow approach of a monarch's vengeance, in the solitary and dismal recesses of the desolate castle in which he was immured, his noble spirit was neither subdued nor depressed. Although separated from his family and friends, and severed as it were from the earth itself; shut out from the light of heaven and the intercourse of man; hearing no sound but the dashing waves against the foundation stones, and the howling of storms among the turrets of his feudal prison, his soul was serene and unruffled, the abode of peace and light.

The kingdom of God is within you, and is the dominion of God in the conscience and spirit of the mind. Those that are in this kingdom . . . have wells and springs open to them in the wilderness, whence they draw out the waters of salvation, without being in bondage to the life of sense.

Common consent, lawfully and rightfully given by the body of a nation, and entrusted with delegates of their own free choice . . . is the principle and means warranted by the law of nature and nations to give constitution and admission to the exercise of government, etc.

Ancient foundations, when they become destructive to the ends for which they were first ordained, and prove hindrances to the good and enjoyment of human societies, to the true worship of God and the safety of the people, are, for their sakes and upon the same reasons, to be altered, for which they were first laid. — *Upham's Life of Sir Henry Vane.*

He hath not spent his life ill that hath learned to die well. — *Meditations at Scilly.*

The spirit of a good man, when he ceases to live in the body, goes into a better state of life than that which he exercises in this world, and when once in that, were it possible to resume this, he would refuse it. — *Meditations at Scilly.*

Blessed be the Lord that I have kept my conscience void of offence unto this day. — *On the Scaffold.*

I have not sought *myself* in any public capacity or place I have been in. — *Sir Henry Vane.*

WILLIAMS.

It is not certain that any one accompanied Williams on his perilous journey on foot through the forests, although a number of persons were with him a few weeks afterwards. With his pocket compass, and a watch to tell the hours, he set out, taking probably the Boston road, over which he had so often travelled to answer the citations of the court, until he reached Saugus, eight or nine miles from his brethren of the Bay, when he may have struck off west for a while, and then due south, until he reached the home of Massasoit, at Mount Hope, near Bristol. The ground was covered with snow, so that he could not resort to roots or fruit to satisfy hunger; and the bringing down game with a heavy matchlock gun imposed a serious burden. Of course he found shelter with friends in the beginning of his tedious walk of eighty or ninety miles, and afterwards with the hospitable natives. Yet he must have suffered severely. In his letter to Major

Mason, he says : " I was sorely tossed for one fourteen weeks in a bitter winter season, not knowing what bread or bed did mean." And in his old age he exclaimed : " I bear to this day in my body the effects of that winter's exposure." — *Footprints of Roger Williams, by Guild.*

The Indians were the ravens that fed me in the wilderness. — *Williams.*

MARQUETTE.

THE 17th of June claims the distinction as being the date of the discovery of the Mississippi River, one hundred and two years before the breaking-out of the Revolutionary War. It was on the 17th of June, 1673, that the eyes of modern civilization first opened upon that mighty stream, — and of course this is what "discovery" really means ; for no account is made in history of the fact that the Father of Waters was ages before paddled over by ignorant savages, who had no literature to report it and no commerce to use it.

The story is that Marquette, a priest, and Joliet, a merchant, with five other Frenchmen and two Indians, left Green Bay, Wis., on the 10th of June, 1673, for a trip to the South-west. Following this direction, they ascended the Fox River in canoes to the head-waters of that stream, in a part of the territory now known as Marquette County, after Father Marquette, the priest.

Aware of a still larger stream west of the ridge of land at the source of Fox River, Joliet and the priest determined to explore further, and dismissed their seven companions to return to Green Bay. The two adventurers carried their light canoe on their shoulders across the "divide" and launched it upon the broad Wisconsin. Travelling rapidly down the current, they soon reached the Wisconsin's mouth, and saw the vast Mississippi spread before them like an inland sea.

Gliding out fearlessly upon its immense waters in their little canoe, the two men continued their voyage southward to the mouth of the Arkansas River, about one hundred and fifty miles below Memphis.

BRADFORD OF AUSTERFIELD.

THE following paragraphs, from an address given at Plymouth on the 262d anniversary of the landing of the Pilgrims, suggested the poem : —

"With full confidence, then, we may rest our thought upon the inclosure of the Scrooby manor-house as 'the cradle of the greatest nation,' — '*maximæ gentis incunabula.*' This is the centre, around which may be drawn the circle, inclusive more or less largely of the neighboring counties, marking the original English home of our Forefathers. The place is one hundred and forty-eight miles north-northwest from London, and seventy-five miles due east from Liverpool. Here, in the connecting years of the sixteenth and seventeenth centuries, Bradford from Austerfield, and Smith, Clifton, Robinson, and others, from various places round about, met together for the worship of God ; an earnest company, — 'whose hearts, 'Bradford says, 'the Lord had touched with heavenly zeal for his truth.'

Here they 'joined themselves (by a covenant of the Lord) into a church estate, in the fellowship of the Gospel.' *The beginning of this nation was in the formation of a church.*

" I commend to your continued thought this wonderful example of loyalty to truth and faith and personal conviction. Especially would I ask you, and in particular you who are in the morning of life, to regard the scene of Bradford himself, not much more than sixteen years old, an orphan boy, daring the ridicule of the rude and profane persons about him, coming down from Austerfield Sabbath after Sabbath, fording the river Ryton, boldly declaring himself a Separatist, making himself an active and useful member of the Scrooby church; thus justifying in his early youth the chiselled record on his monument near by, telling us that he was a 'sincere Christian.' A truly heroic, majestic scene it is. Of what was done by himself, and by the noble company to which he thus allied his destinies, behold the glory; may it embody and reflect itself in all our lives! 'Yea, and the memory of this action shall never die!'

"' For what they were, and all they dared,
Remember them to-day.' "

— *Rev. Geo. A. Tewksbury.*

THE DEATH OF JEFFERSON.

DURING the 3d of July he dozed hour after hour under the influence of opiates, rousing occasionally, and uttering a few words. It was evident that his end was very near, and a fervent desire arose in the minds of all that he should live until the day which he had assisted to consecrate half a century before. He too desired it. At eleven in the evening Mr. N. P. Trist, the young husband of one of his granddaughters, sat by his pillow watching his face, and turning every minute towards the slow-moving hand of the clock, dreading lest the flickering flame should go out before midnight. "This is the Fourth?" whispered the dying patriot. Mr. Trist could not bear to say "Not yet," and so remained silent. "This is the Fourth?" again asked Mr. Jefferson in a whisper. Mr. Trist nodded assent. "Ah!" he breathed, and an expression of satisfaction passed over his countenance. Again he sank into sleep, which all about him feared was the slumber of death. But midnight came; the night passed; the morning dawned; the sun rose; the new day progressed, and still he breathed, and occasionally indicated a desire by words or looks. At twenty minutes to one in the afternoon he ceased to live. — *Parton's Life of Jefferson.*

All eyes are opened or are opening to the rights of man. — *Jefferson, shortly before his death.*

He said, too, that while he feared nothing for our liberty from the assaults of force, he had fears of the influence of English books, English prejudices, English manners, and their apes and dupes among professional men. — *Parton.*

"Patrick Henry" and "Henry Lee." The allusion is to the Virginia House of Burgesses, on instructing its delegates to vote for or sign a Declaration of Independence.

ZINZENDORF.

Jesus, Thy Blood and Righteousness
My beauty are, my glorious dress!
'Midst flaming worlds, in these array'd,
With joy shall I lift up my head.

Bold shall I stand in thy great day,
For who aught to my charge shall lay?
Fully absolved through these I am,
From sin and fear, from guilt and shame.

The holy, meek, unspotted Lamb,
Who from the Father's bosom came,
Who died for me, even me, to atone,
Now for my Lord and God I own.

Lord, I believe thy precious blood,
Which at the mercy-seat of God
For ever doth for sinners plead,
For me — e'en for my soul — was shed.

Lord, I believe were sinners more
Than sands upon the ocean shore,
Thou hast for all a ransom paid,
For all a full atonement made.

When from the dust of death I rise
To claim my mansion in the skies —
E'en then — this shall be all my plea :
Jesus hath lived, hath died for me.

Thus *Abraham*, the Friend of God,
Thus all heaven's armies bought with blood,
Saviour of sinners thee proclaim ;
Sinners, of whom the chief I am.

Jesus, be endless praise to thee,
Whose boundless mercy hath for me,
For me, and all thy hands have made,
An everlasting ransom paid.

Ah ! give to all thy servants, Lord,
With power to speak thy gracious word ,
That all who to thy wounds will flee,
May find eternal life in thee.

Thou God of power, thou God of love,
Let the whole world thy mercy prove !
Now let thy word o'er all prevail ;
Now take the spoils of death and hell.

— Zinzendorf.

[Wesley's Translation.   Written on the return voyage from his
first missionary work in America, in the Antilles.

A man's happiness depends not upon where he
resides, but upon the condition of his heart. *— Zinzendorf, on going into exile.*

That place becomes our home where the most can be done for the Saviour at the time. — *Zinzendorf.*

I have no plan ; I follow Christ from year to year,— I seek out as many of the heathen as I can, I love the pulpit, and I have labored to unite all the children of God who do not dwell together. — *Zinzendorf.*

www.ingramcontent.com/pod-product-compliance
Lightning Source LLC
Chambersburg PA
CBHW022357020726
47500CB00002B/315